The Incident Pit

Chris Leicester

Too Write Productions
Chester, UK

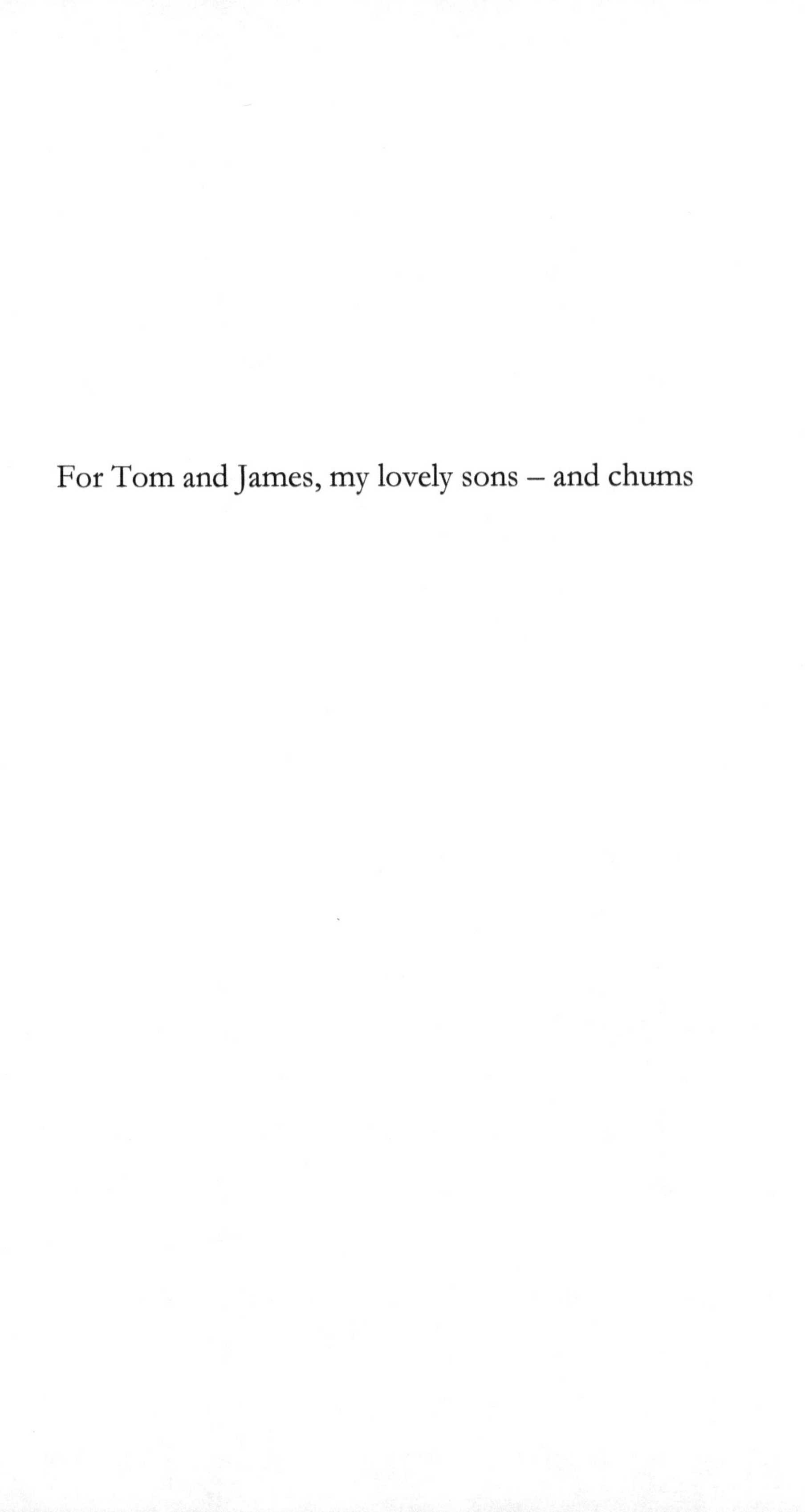

For Tom and James, my lovely sons – and chums

CHAPTER ONE

The 'beep' sounded intrinsically friendly, but perhaps it wasn't. Behind its innocent façade, this was the call of some hideous creature lurking in the shadows, with a soft, inviting, deceptive whistle, beckoning him in. There it was, waiting for him, eyeing his luscious body, eager to rip the flesh from his bones; readying to devour him.

This entity had been present for some time, days actually, relentlessly chirping out its seemingly endless song. It professed to be the voice of survival, and it came in a once regular rhythm, with the spaces between its beats now getting disturbingly longer and longer. But it wasn't so much a warning of a possible fading life, but more a shrill celebration of approaching chaos and death. It was a song everyone was compelled to listen to, but not necessarily the person it watched over. He wasn't able to do that; he couldn't, not in here, as these were the finely tuned vocals of a life support monitor.

The intensive care unit was a very white place. There were no other colours save the shine of the stainless steel beaming from some of the equipment. It was an ordered environment, but cluttered too, with its impressive array of tubes, wires and screens. And it was brilliantly clean. You could almost picture the bacteria as they fled – little specks in a huge, featureless desert, harried by hordes of disinfectant-bearing attackers, leaving them with nowhere to hide. If bacteria could have spoken, you would have heard millions, and then thousands of tiny blood-curdling screams as the friction of cloths and the burning of chemicals destroyed them. In contrast to its décor, the lighting in the room wasn't bright at all. It was subdued, which made this place feel like a hotel room in an expensive, exclusive resort with the last remnants of a paradise island sunset drifting in through the windows.

The digital displays on the equipment were oversized, and the figures they presented were crisp – as if to show their values clearly, and without any delay or ambiguity. Along one wall there was a large window that faced on to the corridor outside. It seemed like whoever was inside this room was on display to the whole world, as if this was some decidedly odd shop, which sold suffering, consequence and catastrophe.

On the solitary, clinical and clever bed lay a patient. He was a man in his early thirties, but the state he was in made him look far older than that. His eyes were closed, and there was no movement in him save the faint rise of his chest from his meagre breathing. His muscular body shaped the otherwise bland, white gown he'd been dressed in, and which had blood seeping through from his left leg. This matched the other patches of red life, which had congealed in his hair, changing it into thick matting. This was darker around the edges, but from its core, a fresh cherry centre appeared like the recently erupted lava from an active volcano.

Back at the monitor, the gaps between the beeps lengthened even further – until they disappeared altogether, and the sound became one continuous string. After ten seconds, an alarm sounded and a bright red light pulsated enthusiastically from the wall above the bedhead. Five seconds after that, the door to the room burst open, and a group of four highly organised people rushed in. A woman in her mid-twenties led the group. She went first to one of the displays.

"He's in arrest," was all she said, a little too calmly, and then, in turn, each of the accompanying party assumed a position around the patient, all tasked with their own duties to fulfil. There were very few words said as they swapped their vital information, figures and read-out data. Then the woman in charge quickly wheeled over a small, grey trolley and took out its contents.

"Clear!"

Her next words rang out like a klaxon, and the others with her stood back as she placed the paddles firmly on the patient's chest. The expression on her face was curious, however. She looked as if she already knew the answer to the question that some of those present might be asking: 'So what of his chances then?' It was as if she was being driven by something non-clinical – gut instinct perhaps; something totally unscientific.

"Clear!" she called again, as she placed the paddles on the patient once more. His body jolted as the charge rippled through it, but the wail of the alarm remained, still loud and ominous; its cutting, sharp song now underscoring the drama that was unfolding unstoppably below its callous gaze.

"Clear!"

She repeated the action one more time, but there was still no reaction from the patient. He remained gaunt and motionless. After ten more seconds, a hand reached over slowly and switched the monitor off. The young doctor looked to the others in the team and shook her head dismally. Then she ushered them out of the room. Once they'd left, she turned to face the now lifeless mass on the bed next to her, and she smiled sadly and affectionately.

"Sorry, love, we did our best," she said to him and then gently closed his eyes.

Outside the room, and some way down the corridor, there was a small and rather desolate-looking waiting area. Here visitors would sit and worry while fate worked its way through things like a scurrying mouse, determining lives and futures.

A woman was sitting there on her own on a battered orange plastic chair which didn't match with anything. A true rebel in the furnishings' world, a James Dean of fixtures, fittings and effects.

She was casually dressed, slightly pretty, with long auburn hair that looked like it needed a good wash. She appeared stressed and pained. She was leaning forwards on the chair, her head thrust into her hands, and she only moved to wipe away the next queuing, dripping tear. People bypassed her, giving her a wide berth as they do when they see such things. Even the medical personnel on their way to somewhere else inserted an immediate banana into their track, bending round, plainly avoiding her immediate vicinity, their eyes now safely planted on an object in the distance giving them an evident excuse not to engage.

Suddenly, by the exit doors twenty or so metres away, a man in his forties tore into view, obviously in a hurry, still in his business suit from the day's toil. He found his footing again, recovering from the spin he'd put himself into. He looked like a dragster at Santa Pod, and when he eventually found traction once more, he looked anxiously about him. He spotted the woman, Fiona, on her tatty chair. He approached her cautiously at first as if she was some stranger he didn't quite recognise. She still didn't move, and he waited patiently beside her for a few seconds before either of them reacted.

"You're too late, Martin," Fiona muttered darkly, not looking up. She faltered on her next words, as if she couldn't believe she was actually speaking them. "He's already gone," she continued unemotionally, but then added with vicious contempt, "But then timekeeping has never been your strong point, has it?"

The man turned away from her instantly; the news she'd imparted evidently hurting him. "Shit," he hissed.

There was a silence where both of them seemed to be taking in the severity of the situation. Still looking away, Martin spoke again.

"What happened?"

Fiona finally sat straight on her chair. She gave her eyes a last wipe.

"No one knows for sure," she explained, coldly. "He had a head injury when they found him on the surface. They think he banged into something. It took a while for anyone to realise he was missing. But it would, wouldn't it?" She eyeballed Martin accusingly. "As nobody knew he was down there."

Martin turned slowly to meet her stare, reluctantly, as if he already knew what to expect, what was coming his way. "When *was* this?"

"This afternoon," Fiona continued soulfully, "or this morning. But I suppose they'll be able to determine that from the autopsy" – now despisingly – "won't they? If it wasn't for his car in the car park, I don't think anyone would've known he was there at all."

"It's not *my* fault he went diving on his own," Martin retorted defensively, becoming visibly more aggressive now.

"Right. But you hardly discouraged him, did you? This bloody obsession you all have."

"It's not an obsession."

"You sure? The 'record' then." Fiona blasted into him mockingly. "*Oh yes.* The first one down to the bottom of some bloody old quarry – is that *really* worth dying for?"

Martin calmed again, and he fixed her with a disabling stare.

"Apparently, yes," he countered. Fiona returned his look, and for a moment the two of them were locked there in the confrontation.

"So why didn't you go with him if you were that 'supportive'?" she asked, persisting with her tone.

"Because he didn't tell me he was going." Martin moved slightly, as if he was seizing the chance to break this awkwardness for both of them. "We'd talked about trying it together. But then there was that rumour about some guys coming over from Stoney to try for it themselves." Martin thought for a moment, like someone does when they're trying to rationalise another's actions. "Maybe he'd heard they were coming over sooner or something. God knows what was in his head. Maybe that swung the odds for him."

Fiona laughed sarcastically.

"'Odds': What, like it's a game of cards or some bloody horse race?"

"It's a dangerous game this; what we do," Martin boomed back. "We all know the rules – including you." Martin moved closer towards her. "You dive too, Fiona, remember?"

"Yes, I do. And you're right; I know it's dangerous. But some of us *don't* know the rules, do we? He should *never* have dived on his own!"

"Well, that's a risk he was obviously willing to take."

"And so it's that easy, is it? There's a reason why it's called 'the Incident Pit'. And now it's claimed yet another life. That's seven in the last five years. Doesn't that mean anything to you?"

"Parachutists jump out of aeroplanes. Racing drivers take bends at a hundred and fifty miles an hour. It's not compulsory. They choose to do it – and they know the risks. We're no different. We do what we do – and we do it there."

"But they still have rules!"

"Which sometimes they break in order to win."

Fiona put her hands to her head in disbelief.

"Are you actually hearing what you're saying?"

Their 'debate' was now gaining the attention of some of the hospital staff further down the corridor, but neither Fiona nor Martin seemed inclined to curtail it.

"Look," Martin pointed angrily at Fiona, "if you don't like what we do then maybe you should take up some other … pastime."

"He was thirty-four," Fiona responded. "He still had his whole life ahead of him. He had a wife and kid for Christ sakes – and what, all that gone – for a dive?"

Martin grinned at her provocatively.

"And that's you speaking for him, is it? You're his official spokesperson now, are you? Are you positive that's what he would have wanted – his epitaph being composed by you of all people? How dare you assume that position!"

"And what exactly do you mean by that?"

"You know precisely what I mean. Rob had balls. He tried things most people could never have even contemplated. You never even liked the guy."

"We had our differences, yes."

"So why are you his 'best mate' then, all of a sudden?"

Fiona caught her breath. She seemed instantly tired. Perhaps the stress and effort of the day had just descended on her with all its full, true weight. Trauma does that. It's like a sleeping dragon. For all the world looking peaceful, regal even. And then in a flash it's up on its feet, belching flames, wanting to destroy that very same world it's just enjoyed so much of that peace in.

She sat back on her misplaced chair again.

"If all of you had listened to me," she resumed; an element of guilt and then anger in her voice, "he might still be here."

Martin stepped deliberately into her personal space once more.

"And so you're the expert as well now, are you?" he demanded, coming at her again, not seeming to care that she was now obviously suffering. "Rob was in this club for nine

years. I've been in it for ten. You've been in it for six months."
He paused momentarily as if searching for the answer to the
question he was about to ask. "Why did you join it, *exactly?*"
Fiona didn't reply. Martin turned his back on her. "Look, go
and get off on somebody else's misfortune," he continued, but
then turned suddenly to face her again. "You could even try
doing it with your own – but you leave Rob alone. Don't piss
on his grave before he's even buried by making this part of
your campaign to champion the unremarkable." Martin moved
to leave, but before he did, he stopped and hurled one last
volley of words at her: "Go and *knit* something, Fiona!" he
bellowed venomously and then carried on his way again. All
Fiona could do was stand and watch as Martin stomped off on
his way.

"I don't bloody believe you!" she cried out after him,
standing again, still not caring about the commotion they were
creating, despite the arrival of a security guard. Martin didn't
react to her comments; instead he punched rather than pushed
open the doors that exited the corridor some distance away.
The doors swung to and fro several times before settling down
to their calmer state once more. Fiona observed them, as they
found their gentleness again, and it was as if that influenced her,
because she now did the same. She felt for and found her basic
plastic seat and slowly lowered herself into it. Seeing her take
this action, the security guard studied her for a moment and
then, seeming happy that there was now nothing to control, he
turned and walked off down the corridor until he was totally
out of view.

CHAPTER TWO

It was 1941, deep in the heart of Germany. Hitler was avidly working on his 'heavy water' project to bring nuclear weapons into the war. Later, the Nazis would abandon their dangerous fascination with fission. They'd adopt the mistaken belief that such technology couldn't provide a killing blow. But at this moment in time, nobody knew of their misguided prediction, and so it had to be assumed that the Germans were planning another mass annihilation; so something had to be done.

The castle stood on its own, on the top of the highest hill for miles, surrounded by forest. It was accessed by a single, lonely track. The building was old and big, and had grand, slim, cylindrical towers, which were capped by ornate, coned, tiled rooves. But that was above ground. Below, in the cellars, things were very different, especially since the SS had commandeered the place. Now part of it was a prison and a place to interrogate the unfortunates they had recently captured.

The other part of the castle, the majority of the space, had been converted to a research facility where large teams worked around the clock, feverishly developing their new, cataclysmic science. The Nazi ideology had spilled out here as it had in many other areas in Europe. It was like an army of ants on the march, destroying and controlling all that lay before it. Many living there scurried or complied, but some stayed and fought. They were like moths perilously perched on the edge of a red-hot crucible, just waiting to be burned. The SS lived well too.

Fine food and wines for the officers, while the locals all around them starved. Their rage of blight and hate was in full flow, and nothing could stop them. It was a truly terrifying time.

The walls of the castle were dug so low they seemed to be leading down to the belly of the earth itself. They were built from huge blocks of stone, and the effort to cut them into shape and then transport them here must have been immense. The structure was designed to be defended, and it would perform that duty admirably. Every so often, as the spiralling steps descended lower still, little rivers of water would trickle down, instilling an instant feeling of numbing coldness in all who saw it. As if to deliberately reinforce this chilling emotion, ice formed in parts, reflecting the advance of the winter, with snow covering the ground many metres above them.

The stairs eventually met a corridor, which then split into two others, and the smaller of them wandered its way for another twenty metres and then abruptly stopped. At this point there was a room, formerly used as a storage area, but now as a place where terror would be applied to induce truth. The SS had secured it with a stout metal door with no windows. A large percentage of its weight was made up of an enormous lock, which would surely have kept dinosaurs out.

The inside of the room was almost a perfect square. Its ceiling was low, and three meagrely lit bulbs trailed off in a line down its centre. There was very little in terms of clutter or furniture, save a couple of chairs and a table. On this lay a variety of instruments; fine for a dentist's surgery or operating theatre perhaps, but not here. This was no such amenity. No health or good intent could ever emanate from this particular space. There were no windows here either, only shadows where demons could have hidden with considerable ease, looking on, gloating; gratefully witnessing the atrocities.

In front of the table, one of the chairs was placed on its own, a notable distance away. It was stout and functional with a cold metal seat and sturdy legs. It was more like shelving than something to sit comfortably on. But then its purpose was wildly disconnected from any kind of rest or relaxation.

In this chair sat a young woman. Her hands were tied behind her back with an over-thick rope that wound its way through the furniture's cross-members. She was in her early twenties, and she was very attractive. She wore dirty-looking, old, brown trousers; like a farm worker might wear. Her hair fell down around her shoulders. A section of it was missing, suggesting she'd been manhandled and pulled by it in a preceding struggle. Her old coat had been ripped from her and it lay, cast away some metres away on the floor. Her thick, rough, green-coloured, agricultural shirt was speckled with blood, and her lower lip was cut. The door behind her opened.

She looked anxiously in its direction as she heard the painful groan of its rusting hinges. Then it closed again. There were no footsteps at first. Whoever had entered waited, studying, planning perhaps, and then the clump of heavy-heeled boots began. Six long, straight, determined steps and then the silhouette of a figure loomed out of the blackened space and manifest by her side.

This was a man. He was surprisingly young; more her age, and yet he carried a senior rank. The young woman picked at his image as best she could in the dull light, obviously her training forcing her to take snippets of information whenever she could; her bright, alert eyes gathering far more than he could possibly have anticipated.

As he moved fully into the light, she could see that he was quite good-looking. Who knows the cruelty of fate? In another scene, in another kinder time, maybe they could have been presented as a couple; students meeting on their travels on a gap year; man and wife even, matched perfectly, exploring enthusiastically what was yet to be. But this was not the case. This was not that kinder time.

Suddenly the man leaned in, close to her face. The young woman didn't flinch. He smiled at her before he spoke.

"We can do what we like, when we like, and to whoever we like," he said, his voice calm and intrusive. "We can take lands and lives, and no one can stop us." He seized her chin and pulled her forcibly round to face him, so she strained on her bonds and winced a little as the rope bit into her wrists. "When are you people going to realise this?" he sneered.

The SS officer stepped away from her and gazed up at one of the spartan bulbs for a while.

"All your accomplices are dead," he continued, still facing away from her. "One of them told us you were farm workers before her shoddy German slipped and gave her away." He turned back and grinned satisfactorily. "You were harder to find. Dressing as a man was clever." He looked her up and down. "But there was something about the way you walked that wasn't quite right. We know why you're here. This facility has been of great interest to the British for some time now. But why wouldn't it be?"

He leaned against the table, as if showing the young woman how comfortable he felt and how his state was in obvious contrast to her own.

"The others died before they could tell us who helped you." He stood straight again and moved towards her, slowly and menacingly as he spoke. "We know it's the Resistance, but we need to know *who* exactly. We need to minimise future … risks. I'm sure you understand."

Now in front of her again, he took her face in his hand, harder this time, and pulled her towards him.

"Are they really worth suffering all that pain for?" He grinned. "Because there *will* be pain … and mutilation … and disfigurement. You'll never be able to have children – pity." He eyed her grotesquely. He stroked her cheek and then kicked her legs apart and leered at her disgustingly. "Such a shame." Then he bent down, so their faces were level and just a few centimetres apart. "But it won't be *what* we're going to do to you that'll make you want to tell us all we need," he went on. "No, it'll be the *fear* of what we're going to do to you that will see to that. That's the greater force here, you see; the trigger in your brain. It'll sit inside you and grow like a cancer or a parasite, consuming you exponentially, biting, dissolving, breaking you down, changing you; making you *decide.*" He licked her cheek like a lion does before it takes a bite from its freshly brought-down prey. "Yes, *fear* is the thing," he said.

CHAPTER THREE

The series of ladders which the driver used to climb to the cab would have reached up to the second storey of most houses, but they looked almost tiny here, connected to the side of the radiator on this massive motorised monster. But then, they still only reached halfway up its height. Everything was huge on this machine, with even its model number implying some enhanced scale. It wasn't just a '7D' or a '78D', but a 'Caterpillar 789D', the numerals moving away from the singular and encroaching on the thousands quite readily, marking the increase in size.

The Caterpillar was a giant truck that was used in the quarry before it closed in 1985. It was one of a fleet of eight, which carried slate and waste material from the bowels of the site up to the surface and the processing plant beyond. It was powered by a 2100 horse-power diesel engine and could carry 178 tons on its back on every trip. It wasn't particularly slow either. It could zip along at a respectable pace, but it would slurp down a small lake of fuel as it did so. Its 4.5-metre diameter tyres cost thousands each and had to be specially constructed to cope with its frighteningly heavy loads.

The driver was housed in the cab situated midway up the front of the truck. This was square and was relatively small compared to the rest of the design. It was like looking at a disfigured face; the creator of everything having an off-day, the Friday afternoon shift when they were rushed or couldn't be bothered. It was a very small nose on a great big face. It wasn't until you studied it more deeply, that it was obvious the cab itself was quite large, with the operator of this machinery appearing as a comparative speck inside it, such were this colossus's dimensions.

The interior of the quarry was like one of those plastic fish-pond liners people use in their back gardens. They're usually an odd, oval shape, steep-sided in parts with undulations and plateaus that extend down to their base. The quarry was virtually the same design, but it was over three miles wide and three hundred metres deep. And to get down to those depths where the freak carp and snails might have lived, roads had been constructed that circled patiently down, cut out of, and then clinging to, the edges of the indigenous rock.

On these roads, there was two-way traffic. Empty trucks going down would squeeze past full trucks coming up, and to their side there were almost certain death category drops. They were like long-term members of Slimming World at their regular weekly meet, passing each other on the stairs of the building – one going up to get weighed and the other coming down, looking dejected yet again, wishing they just hadn't been.

The traffic here was frequent and heavy too, and this was beginning to show on the road's surface and, markedly, at its edges which were now dangerously tatty. In sections, clear lines – between where the road ended and where space began – were difficult to determine. If it was raining or occasionally misty, picking out these vital definitions through a spattered and dusty windscreen was quite some skill – and such had been the challenge today.

This truck had managed most of the climb from the quarry floor easily enough. Now, almost at the top, and at one of the thinnest sections of the road, it faced another leviathan coming the other way. They were like two advancing elephants treading the same restricted, greasy path.

Perhaps the differences in experience between the two drivers should have accounted for what happened next, but things had turned upside down a little. One of them had years under his belt, and was familiar with every turn and twist of the quarry, but the other was a recent recruit; he'd spent some time over in Australia in the quarries there, but their sizes at this time were nothing compared with the dimensions of this place. Spare room for extravagant manoeuvres or errors weren't luxuries that were afforded here. There were no vast accommodating red trails where the trucks could almost drive themselves. This disparity in environments was about to present itself in a dangerous and spectacular form.

Given the rules of flow, the least experienced driver had to take the outer track. As he rumbled closer to the edge, he looked nervously through his cab window down on to the seemingly unending depths below. He was like an acrophobic who suddenly finds himself inside the basket of a hot air balloon that's floating 4,000 feet off the ground.

Seeing the approaching truck, he moved over another half metre, but apparently that wasn't enough for the opposing driver – as he signified with an angry wave of his arm.

"Shift it!" he screamed at his windscreen, and the nervous driver duly obliged.

Some way up the road the foreman looked on. He'd recently been rocketed by the management for letting output figures slip, and his middle-aged face was rippled with stress. He immediately spotted the trucks and observed their mechanical face-off with more than some concern.

With the oncoming truck still not giving him the space he demanded, the arrogant driver continued his altercation through his cab window – but more ferociously now. His intimidation was clearly working because the less experienced driver nudged over a few more inches. The foreman watched as the driver continued his track. Now the foreman's face changed and an expression of pure horror took over it.

"No!" he yelled, and set off running up the road towards the two trucks, but he was too late. "Get out!" the foreman commanded, bawling at the rookie driver. "You're going off the edge!"

Without hesitating, the rookie opened his cab door, negotiated the cold and unforgiving metal steps of the ladders and hurled himself headlong on to the ground. With his foot now off the accelerator, his huge charge trundled to a stop, half of its rear wheel hanging over the cliff. With the weight from its load bearing down, the edge of the road began to crumble like a sandcastle caught by the first waters of an incoming tide. More and more of the edge fell away until the truck eventually thankfully stopped. Now it sat crooked and angled, threatening to plunge to the quarry floor hundreds of feet below at any moment.

The rookie driver wandered around the road, looking useless and confused as if he was trying to figure out what to do next. When the foreman bounded up to him, he looked frightened and backed away, as if he was expecting violence of some kind. But the foreman left him alone and marched on towards the other driver, who was now looking down through the safety of his cab window.

"You fucking idiot!" the foreman shrieked up at him, "You had acres to spare!"

The arrogant driver didn't respond, rather he found a gear, revved his engine and prepared to move off.

"No, you don't!" the foreman roared, pointing threateningly at him. "You bloody well stay here!"

The driver took his foot off the gas as he mumbled to himself. Then, seeing the lasering glare from the foreman, he suddenly averted his gaze, leaned back to be out of view, and skulked into the apparent sanctuary of his seat. The foreman advanced further on to him, raging now, when there was a disabling sound, which stopped him dead in his tracks.

The rear tyre of the rookie's truck let out a deep wrenching noise as the whole machine lurched another two inches over the void. This broke the exchange between the two men, and now the foreman looked about him, frantically searching for a solution to this horrendous predicament.

The foreman stood on the road, studying the scene for a while to the accompaniment of the engine of the marooned truck, which was still running.

"Sorry," its driver muttered to him as he sidled carefully over, finally approaching like a mischievous little kid. The foreman looked at him surprisingly caringly.

"Don't worry about it, John," he replied, sounding kind even now. "That arsehole should have given you more room. I've told the stupid bastard about that before. Trouble is that sump," he said, suddenly sounding more concerned, and nodding over to the truck. "The oil collectors'll not pick anything up with her being at an angle like that." He thought hard for a moment, and then quickly moved off.

"Where are you going?" John called after him, his voice riddled with alarm.

"To turn her off."

"But she could go at any moment!"

The foreman stopped and turned back to face John for a few seconds.

"If that block seizes, I'll be fucked," he declared. "It's been a bad enough week as it is," he cursed, and hurriedly set off again.

The foreman took care with placing his steps as he walked towards the machine. It was as if any vibration, no matter how small, might bring on a calamity. Tens of thousands of pounds sent down to oblivion by the merest shuffle. From a metre away, he stopped and studied, picking his spot, like a snake-charmer assessing his charge, conscious of a strike and the subsequent doom. He placed one foot on the base of the ladder first, and carefully tried his weight. Then, with one smooth, graceful movement, he was aboard. As he looked on, the arrogant driver sank further into his seat with a tangible sheen of guilt plastered liberally over his face. But then, without warning, the rookie's truck started to move again.

"Shit!" the foreman hissed, and abandoning any further caution, he scampered up the steps, burst into the cab, sat in the driver's seat and gently dabbed the brakes. The truck calmed and halted again, like a slumbering giant unwittingly disturbed but then mercifully falling back to sleep once more. The foreman sat there for a moment, his face red, his heart pounding as it almost burst through his chest. He had a walkie-talkie in the top pocket of his jacket, which he gingerly took out.

"Billy, are you there?" he asked meekly, speaking into it.

"Yes, boss," came a light-hearted reply. Obviously, Billy didn't fully realise what was happening further on into the quarry.

"Look, Billy," the foreman carried on, "I've got a bit of a problem up on twenty-six. Can you bring the chains up pronto, mate?"

"No sweat," Billy answered. "But is that a 'problem' problem or just a problem?"

"No, it's a 'problem', I'm afraid – and a right fucking big one. We've got a machine that's over the edge of the road. I've now got to leave the engine running in case we need the brakes again. But she's on a slant, so we've got to watch the crank too; so time's a bit short if you know what I mean."

"Right. Then I'll be with you as soon as I can."

"Oh, and Billy."

"Yeah?"

"You might want to start clearing a way through further down the levels just in case my plan doesn't work. Talk to people; get 'em clear, eh?"

"Bollocks. It *really* is a problem then?"

"Oh aye, and that it is."

The battered old Land Rover arrived two minutes later, fighting up the road like an elderly but resilient runner with heavy breaths and a sometimes shaky pace. Billy jumped athletically out of it without speaking to anyone. He went straight to the rear of the vehicle and dropped down the low gate that accessed the flatbed behind the cab. Lying on the tough base was a thick spaghetti of metal chains, and on each end, there was a huge hook with a heavy clasp that locked them in place. Billy grabbed the nearest tail, and the apparent impossibly knotted length obligingly slid out to form one rather pleasing straight strip.

"Where do you want it?" he asked the foreman who had joined him at his side. The hook was cradled in Billy's arms like some odd, troublesome, overweight baby. The foreman nodded over to the crippled, teetering truck.

"On the U," he said, and without waiting for any more instructions, Billy strode over, the chain following behind him, and he placed the hook around a stout metal U-shaped bar which was welded to the lower part of the chassis on the giant. The metal here was around 30 cm thick and was designed as a towing lug. Once it was secured, Billy trailed back down the length of the chain and laid it on the ground, ready for the next stage of his impromptu rescue mission. The arrogant driver shuffled in his seat, readying to restart his truck, picking up what was about to happen next.

"No!" the foreman shouted up. "Not you!"

"But it's my truck," the driver protested childishly through the glass of his cab.

"Not any more it isn't. Get down!" the foreman snarled, and transferred his line of sight to the rookie driver. "Your turn," he ordered. "Come on," the foreman continued, sensing the reluctance in his shaken employee. "I'm in this one. I can't be soddin' everywhere." The foreman smiled considerately. "Just keep on your talkie, listen to what I tell you and everything will be fine."

The once terrified driver now seemed bolstered by this seemingly reckless act of trust the foreman was placing in him. This must have worked because the rookie marched over to the other truck, climbed up the ladder and promptly got in. Its former driver murmured to himself. He swore as he walked away some distance down the road, his head lowered, clearly sulking. Once in the driver's seat, the machine's new operator throttled up the mighty engine and held his walkie-talkie close to his ear, waiting for orders. The foreman spoke into his handset as he calculated the measurement between the two huge monsters.

"Come on, bring her forward ten more feet," he instructed.

The rookie duly reacted to his words, nudging the truck closer to the edge of the road. The foreman raised his hands and the driver stopped. Billy connected the other hook on the chain to the second truck. Then he stood straight again and quickly took a big, precautionary step backwards away from the danger.

"Take up the slack!" the foreman boomed. The second truck nudged backwards, and the massive links in the chain bit into each other – an odd, dull, low ring emanating from the bulk of them as they did so. The foreman spoke into his walkie-talkie once again.

"Let's get her out exactly the way she went in – backwards," he said, enunciating his words precisely into his microphone. "You pull me back and I'll follow the same tracks out. Okay?"

"Got it," the rookie answered, the enthusiasm in his voice indicating how pleased he was to be helping now.

"Good. Then let's do it," the foreman continued. "When I've got my reverse gear, I'll give you the word and then you move us an inch at a time; gent-ly. You bloody understand?"

"One inch at a time," the other driver repeated. "Just give me the word when you're ready."

The foreman paused for a moment before boarding his truck. He looked up at it, as if he was peering into the future itself, as if there was an alternative world residing in the metalwork and paint. Then, when he was finally ready, he climbed nimbly but carefully on to the truck and then into its cab, in one swift and effective arc of his body. He resembled a monkey travelling effortlessly up a tree. The engine revved and then he spoke into his handset.

"Right. Go," he directed calmly, and the other truck began to snort and nudge backwards like a cornered bull. "That's it; keep it going," the foreman encouraged, and his truck did quite well to begin with. The rear wheels began to move back on to the safety of the road, and as they did so, the truck began to right itself. And then that terrifying call:

"She's going, she's going!" the rookie screamed. "Move! Get the fuck out of there!"

A large and uncompromising slab of slate suddenly began to move under the back wheels of the foreman's truck, as it fought to find its feet on sturdier ground. The slab was of such a size that it was almost like a small road in itself. The wheels of the truck had no chance at all. Gone was the opportunity to fingernail this, to grasp and creep back bit by bit, to reconnect with a stable surface. A whole chunk of the edge of the road was collapsing now, and nothing could stop its fall.

The door of the cab flew open, and the foreman vaulted over the rails, ignoring the steps. Finding the rubber of the slightly turned nearside front wheel, he slid on his buttocks down its tread and then clumsily on to the ground. He landed heavily, but his first instinct seemed to be the safety of the rookie driver. He'd now slammed on his brakes and was racing his engine hard in reverse as the gigantic wheels started sliding across the road closer to the drop beyond, pulled on by its poor, unfortunate brother. The far wheels of this, both back and front, were now hanging over the plunging face below. The towing machine started to roll forward and as it did so, gravity joined in the party, accentuating and magnifying the effect of the weight and its resultant, potential, unspeakable consequence.

"Get out!" the foreman bellowed to the rookie. "Just go!"

The rookie tried again to hold the mass in front of him which was now slithering over the cliff like some massive, bizarre blancmange. And it was then when the chain snapped. Unable to cope with such a severe amount of tonnage, a link severed and shot skywards as it shattered. The foreman and Billy ducked as they heard it go, as if they were waiting for shrapnel from the blast of a hand grenade. The other truck lurched backwards, now free of its ward, which went spinning down to the bottom of the quarry. Level by level it went, thumping down, somersaulting, amazing the people who were watching it go. It clipped a large supply shed halfway down, shattering its corner and catapulting the corrugated sheeting from its roof into the air like huge playing cards ejected from their pack. The carcass of the truck eventually came to rest upside down, mutilated, and wedged on to the unforgiving crest of a mountainous rock. This rock had survived many attempts to shift it by dynamiting over the years, and this relatively small toy, which it now wore on its head, would hardly alter that situation.

The foreman and Billy peered over the edge of the road, looking on through the dust and commotion below. The foreman rubbed his hands through his hair, his face already pained by the thoughts of the forthcoming anguish he would surely receive by having to explain all this. The rookie driver appeared by his side next to Billy.

"You all right?" the foreman asked him. The driver nodded.

"Yeah."

"Good," the foreman answered, sounding relieved. "Bollocks to this," he continued. "Let's go and have a fucking cup of tea."

The resources of the earth have to be fought for. That was true just as much here as in any location in the world. The soul of the land isn't ripped out without it putting up a fight. And the quarry didn't disappoint. Fourteen lives were lost during the time the facility operated commercially. The place had a 'personality', some of the former workers had stated. As spirits leave a residual presence in old houses, then a 'person' lived here in the quarry too, many believed. It was like nature's voice, its representative; a warrior fighting against all that had been violated, taken, stolen from it. It was the protector of the place, and it would remain here for ever, long after the quarry had closed and, in its current form, ceased to be.

CHAPTER FOUR

It was an odd setting. Due to a shortage of space, they now used the magistrates' courts for such events, and so anyone entering the building was subject to that same scowl by the attending officials, that judgemental look; implying they were immediately guilty of some crime or other. It was a weird application of logic, and it made those entering who were not accused of anything, feel obliged to prove they weren't. This was reinforced by the contradiction in what the inquest stated as its function. It wasn't its job to apportion blame it said, but to all outside appearances, given where it was being held, that's exactly what it seemed to be doing.

The building was relatively new; built in the late 2000s by the look of it. They'd taken the time to help it blend into its neighbours, with its intricate brickwork and attractive pitched roof. It had a spread of steps shaped like an opened fan leading up to its entrance. It hatched a kind of expectation as you approached it, with a mixture of both grandeur and fear oozing from it. But then as you did enter, you were greeted by a grubby A4 typed sheet, sellotaped to the inside of the glass, with the instruction: 'USE SIDE DOOR'. Underneath this impoliteness, a hand-drawn thick, black, wobbly arrow pointed right.

Inside, there were tight, metal security arches through which everybody had to pass, including the magistrates who entered with their over-important, pompous faces lifted skywards. At either side of the arches there were little black tables. The nearest one to the door was set with what looked like a seedling tray, into which you placed anything metal. Once you'd walked through and been scanned for anything dangerous, then your tray would follow, and you'd be asked to reassemble yourself. Beyond the arches, there was a solitary reception desk built into the wall, with bulletproof glass protecting its inner, fuller space. For communication, there was an inadequate screened grill into which people had to shout. From there you'd be directed to wherever you'd been ordered to be, usually up to one of the four courts, which were housed in the expansive two-storey building.

Court Number Two was where they'd all gathered. The place was packed, and the supply of seats set aside for the public had been exhausted ages ago. In a separate section sat members of the press. There were five of them in total, all with notepads and pens which were eagerly waiting to be connected with each other.

Outside this court were the entrances to the other courts. Their spillage of anxious attendees collected in little pockets, and the whole scene was an intriguing blend of those waiting for the coroner's court; the yet-to-be-proven guilty, the about-to-be-discharged, witnesses, members of the authorities who wanted some of the number there caged, and members of the legal profession who wanted some of them freed. The remainder were a mish-mash of miscellaneous, extraneous court administrators and the morbidly curious.

The coroner had already entered to an acquiescent bow from the court officials who occupied the long line of wooden benches in front of her – high and aloft, above everybody both in authority, status and capacity. But today this was *her* court, after all.

She was middle-aged, rather portly and had a round face, on which were perched a disproportionately small pair of reading glasses. She had a somewhat comedic look about her as a result, and she appeared far too jolly for where they all found themselves now, and the proceedings they were about to face. It seemed a real effort for her to sustain her serious expression, which was so intense it looked like a mask.

After ten minutes, the introductions had been made, the purpose of the inquest detailed, and the first witnesses called. These were comprised of various policemen and some bureaucrat from the Health and Safety Executive. Then it was time for members of the dive club to give their accounts. The secretary had spoken first about how they conducted their business, what systems they had and how they recorded things. The coroner jumped in with various pertinent questions as they seemed to occur to her and nodded patiently as her answers followed. Then she explained that it was time for colleagues and friends of the deceased to give their accounts too, but 'from a more personal perspective' as she described it and Martin was next up to the stand.

Martin stood squarely in the dock, and then his shoulders drooped. He looked emotional as he took a minute to gather his thoughts. He glanced briefly around at the silenced, keen, expectant faces out beyond him.

"I've talked about Rob in many places," he began, "but I never thought I'd be talking about him from the witness stand of a coroner's court." He faltered for a moment, stuck there like a car, its engine screaming, fighting to find the right gear. The coroner picked up on his discomfort and intervened.

"Why don't you start by telling us what he was like?" she suggested kindly. Martin regained his composure and carried on.

"Rob was fearless; daring." Martin smiled slightly with affection. "He was an adventurer, phenomenally physically fit and as hard as nails. He was ex-services." Pride flickered across his face. "He'd been to places, done things that some of his best mates still don't know anything about." He slowed again, sounding as if he was talking about someone who was extremely close to him – like someone who was talking about a favourite brother. "He was loyal, compassionate, generous, stubborn, loving;" – he grinned – "funny." Martin looked directly at the coroner now. "And he took risks," he went on. "Rob was that pioneer in a waggon train battling across the Wild West, fighting off the Indians, drinking the whiskey, enjoying the moment; living life to the full."

Martin paused now. He looked suddenly sterner, even accusatory. The court picked up on this, and there was an obvious, collective mass-shuffling forwards on seats, so no one missed anything.

"But then there's another person in this story too, isn't there?" Martin continued eventually. "That's what it feels like anyway; *real*, with a personality and qualities all of their own." He pointed out into the court. "That quarry, that place – the Incident Pit." He slowed again, looking directly at his audience for a few seconds. "I couldn't talk about Rob without talking about that too."

Martin altered his position in the witness stand, getting more comfortable, evidently settling in like a story-teller does, ahead of their gripping tale.

"It's huge; miles wide," Martin began again, a hint of wonder in his eyes now. "One of those places you can see from space, probably. Given its size and challenges, it's been used as a dive site for decades now; an irresistible draw. But if this place truly is a person, then we should label it a murderer. There've been lots of casualties. Last year it claimed three lives in one month alone. The local paper ran a front-page headline which read: 'Stop This Madness'".

Martin ceased speaking momentarily, as if he was assessing the reaction of those listening, checking to see if they were taking his words seriously. He seemed content that they were, and so he resumed.

"The first two dangers of the Pit are easy enough to understand. It's cold and incredibly deep. In winter the water's close to ice – just three degrees. But then there's a third danger; 'attitude', and that's when the real trouble begins."

Martin looked down at the structure of the stand in which he stood. He paused as if he was recounting its history for a moment; who else had been there, why and what had happened to them. It was as if a multitude of completely separate lives suddenly came alive there in front of him, united by a common experience of being forced into that space and ordered to speak. The residual energy generated by all those episodes, which were saturated in fear and emotion, seemed to affect Martin for a time, flood over him, disabling him almost, stemming the flow of his words. After a number of impossibly long seconds of silence for everyone, he finally broke his gaze from the dull, wooden, stained edging ahead of him and focused on the broader aspect of the court once more.

"The recommended safe dive limit is fifty metres down," he carried on. "But there are people who dive to one hundred metres. Some dive to one hundred metres, hold their breath and dive even further down. The …" – he hesitated slightly as he fought with one particular word, as if he was finally acknowledging its power, and its relevance – "… 'obsession' this quarry has created is there because this site has never been fully dived. The bottom in one section has never been reached. It's unexplored, unconquered, and so some kind of glory awaits those who finally feel that sand, touch that rock. The problem is, that place could lie one hundred and thirty metres down, or more." Martin smiled slightly. There was almost a flash of joy across his face now. "A new part of the planet is just waiting to be discovered, right here on earth. Now who wouldn't want their name on that, I wonder?"

The coroner nodded ever so gently, as if she understood Martin's reasoning, at least in part. This caught the attention of those in the public gallery and then Martin's attention in turn. He waited for her to conclude her display and then proceeded, but now with a more serious tone in his voice.

"But the word 'economics' should be added to this equation too," he said. "Because of all the 'carnage', the agencies want to ban diving in the quarry altogether – and to legislate for it too. So now we have market forces in play. Something is becoming rare. So, ironically, measures to control 'recklessness' by record-seeking divers, only serve to drive that recklessness on. They've added one of the most potent ingredients you could ever put into a situation – time – or the lack of it. Now we have the consequences of rationing. The authorities have unwittingly created a kind of panic buying for adventurers. The record for the Pit has become a Holy Grail. The image of a closing door makes people do apparently insane things. They're driven to act before the hinges squeak, the frame is filled by the wood, the latch is turned, and the door is banged shut for ever, never to open again."

Martin's face took on a sudden expression of sadness, like a dull, grey primer wash on a watercolour painting.

"Rob was a victim of these market forces," Martin continued, "and, I'm afraid to say, there will undoubtedly be others who will be influenced too, corrupted by time, infected, smitten; taken by the 'madness' of the Incident Pit." Martin became instantly bolder, as if he was being stronger, not just for himself, but for someone else too. He smiled kindly. "Rest in peace, mate," he said softly, "rest in peace."

CHAPTER FIVE

The clubhouse didn't seem any different from before, but perhaps it should have because so much had happened. It felt empty now. The heating was turned off and it was cold inside. It seemed barren in there, lifeless almost.

The building itself was a well-used, portable construction. It was still hanging on to the town planners' definition of 'temporary' with extreme optimism. It still functioned, however. It did its job splendidly and was dearly loved by all the members of the dive club who frequented it. It was like an ill relative. Everyone gave it space, made allowances; remembered it how it used to be.

It wasn't small either. It was situated on a plot some sixty metres square. It had a concrete base upon which an old quarry building had originally sat. This wooden structure had been craned in during the early 1990s, when it had looked quite modern. It had main double doors which were positioned right in the middle of the building's thirty-metre length. Once in, the accommodation was distributed equally to a small office, training room and storage area to the left, and clubhouse to the right.

This was a cosy space, with old sofas spread around the walls, avoiding the draughty windows. There was a limited kitchen where meals could be cooked, and drinks made to warm chilled divers when they returned from the water. In one corner, there was an old and rather grubby wood-burning stove, courageously placed close to the wooden wall. The material here had not ignited in the many years the fire had been working, which suggested that, given this rather ambitious test, the stove was safe to use and so could remain.

Out through the rear of the building, mirroring the doors in, there was another entrance leading out to steps which trickled down to a compact, sandy beach. Around its fringes were several rustic table and bench units with holes set in their centres to stabilise sun umbrellas when the weather was nicer. Beyond the beach was the quarry itself, looking imposing, and today, dull. A light mist had gathered someway off over the surface of the water, and it would have been easy to have imagined some fine, old, ghostly galleon appearing out of the gloom. The beach dropped gradually, and then suddenly. Set in its centre, following this incline, was a cement pathway a metre or so wide, which wandered off into the distance; this was the route club members followed as they headed off into the depths.

Back inside the unit, a figure sat on the best of the sofas holding a mug of the finest coffee she could find. As she wrapped her fingers tightly around it, eager to share its warmth, the sofa seemed to afford her the same kindness, enveloping her in its deep and friendly cushions.

Fiona stared out into space as she took another sip. And then she spoke.

"It feels odd without him around," she muttered, almost deliberately mournfully. After a while, another voice sounded out from over by the nearest window.

"I didn't expect to see you here," Martin commented, holding a mug too. "It's only been a week."

He didn't move as he spoke. Like Fiona, he remained motionless. It was as if the whole building had been forced into a period of compulsory meditation. A nesting crow in a tree just outside was bickering with one of its neighbours, its cry imitating automatic gunfire. Fiona and Martin both looked up, startled a little, but then having identified what it was, they returned to their former state of torpor again. Fiona was the first to break the moment as she pivoted her head to look at Martin. She settled on his face, examining his features as if she was checking for changes there, for evidence of any differences. Then she spoke to him again, almost with nonchalance now.

"I've come to pack my things," she said, with no hint of emotion in her voice. Martin broke out of his daze immediately.

"What?" he asked in disbelief. He began to move away from the window to be closer to her.

"I'm leaving the club, Martin," Fiona clarified and then she smiled cynically. "*Why* do we let people go to their deaths?" she ruminated accusingly.

On hearing these words, Martin made a change to his plans. He stopped his advance, put down an anchor. He shook his head slightly and his expression became a billboard for his inner thoughts. It carried the slogan: *'Oh God, not this again'*. Fiona rumbled on despite him, fixing on something mid-room that wasn't there, pursuing her self-examination.

"It's been eating into me all week," she resumed, her face twisted now, as if her anguish was so strong it was physically contracting her muscles. "Logically, really? I mean, if we know they might die; why do we let them go? Why do they let *us* let them go? I can't rationalise it any more. Why do we dive? All that risk? A world hardly anyone will ever see and so appreciate, all that cold and discomfort." She glared at Martin now with a penetrating stare. "Why?"

Martin pondered for a time before answering her. He played around with the tea in his mug, swishing it around in a little whirlpool, as if now, given the situation he found himself in, he actually preferred its company.

"All of the above, possibly," he replied, while still facing away from Fiona as if he couldn't bear to look at her, as if he was tired of her. "But try adding 'magnificent', 'beautiful' and 'privileged' as well."

Fiona huffed dismissively, quietly and annoyingly, but loud enough so that Martin could pick up her intention.

"All very poetic," she scoffed.

Martin creased his face up, clearly vexed.

"Do you not get it?" he asked her. "Staring death right in the face keeps people alive. It's like my Hayabusa."

Fiona reeled.

"Great. Your damn bike again."

"Yes, my damn bike, my 'Busa'. It's the same thing. I love the fact it can do a hundred in first gear, that it's got a top speed of two hundred …"

"Well, good for you …"

"Exactly." Martin took a step closer to her to emphasise his point. "And that not everyone is allowed to ride one." He held there for a few seconds watching his words filter into her, waiting for a reaction. But there was none. More softly now, he moved back, returned her space to her and panned out a scene with broad strokes of his hands in front of them. "It's a chilly autumn day," he went on, a smile of appreciation accompanying his words. "We're kitted out; we're about to get in the boat, we're ready, armed; like warriors. But it's the expressions on the faces of the people who are with me that get to me the most. They conquer fear – or at least they conquer the control it has over them. They've committed to the adventure; they're in."

Seemingly already tiring of his instant lecture, Fiona sneered.

"Right, and so where does that leave Rob, exactly?"

"Having done it," Martin replied, replicating her blunt tone. "Come on, tell me you can't still remember your first big dive? Tell me it didn't affect the way you lived the rest of your life after completing it? Barriers broken, frontiers crossed; a whole new attitude?" He paused as he recalled a time fondly. "I can still remember mine. I was out in the Solomon Islands at the time. The two guys I were with were already in the water; that beautiful, crystal-clear water; me nervous, still in the boat. I looked down, and I could see Matt sitting crossed-legged on the seabed thirty metres below, beckoning me down. There was just no other way. I had to get on with it."

Martin nodded slowly, looking at the floor, the images in his head taking over completely now. "The wrecks, the three-thousand-foot drop-off; the first fish I saw was a lion fish. We even discovered a new reef. Then, all that followed; the barracuda, the Japanese supply ship still with a tank and ammunition in its hold. A Mitsubishi Zero sat on the bottom in the sand where it had crash-landed after being shot down. It concluded with me seeing a killer whale. I returned to the surface half-comatose with all that wonder crammed into my head." He broke from his recollection and addressed Fiona squarely now. "I've never forgotten that, and I never will. Having been there, having seen what is possible *has* guided my life ever since – and I'm still extremely grateful for that."

Martin turned away now as if he needed to rest, his display of enthusiasm obviously draining him. Fiona stood and moved to look out through one of the windows, still largely ignoring him. Twenty metres or so away, a moorhen was scuttling across the water – half-flying, half-running like they do – seeking safety from any killers up above who might be looking down. After a dash of a few seconds, the moorhen found its nest, which was tucked into the twisted, fortressed roots of a hawthorn tree. In the nest was another moorhen, its mate probably, and they nuzzled briefly but subtly as they came together, complete now with the protection from their tree and, as best as they could muster, the protection they offered for each other.

"All this has made me think too," Fiona began again, targeting her words more to the world outside and herself rather than to this man inside the room with her now. "What about children, Martin?"

"What about them?"

Fiona faced Martin again, shaking her head slightly in disbelief.

"Neither of us have any. Or haven't you noticed?"

"I know we don't, and perhaps that's why danger's possible for us in the first place."

"But don't you ever want a *different* kind of danger; the … *softer* kind?"

Martin thought. "No, I don't," he replied sounding as cold as ice. "Not yet anyway."

Fiona found her mug again and admired it fondly. She took another thankful sip, and although her drink was cooling rapidly by now, this odd friendship was readily sealed. As she held her mug, her thoughts wandered off to somewhere else as her memories appeared to take over her. It was a kinder, distracting place, something summoned by her soul to support her. Like a considerate parent might take their six-year-old to the toy shop ahead of that dental appointment that is always dreaded. They purposely instil some pleasantness to counter the misery and fear that's lying ahead of their child. None of it is required, but yet it's willingly done.

"Someone brought their baby into the office last week," Fiona went on. "Just three weeks old. Sleeping soundly, he was. He didn't cry as she placed him in my arms. It felt *so* wonderful just to hold him for those vital few seconds."

The office had been cleaned for once. Some gesture by the management to improve working conditions, boost morale and bolster performance. But this hadn't worked. The people who worked there were still just the same. They were just normal human beings with hopes, expectations and influences. And it was a Monday, and these were always the worst days. This was

when the inboxes and answering machines would need
emptying after the weekend's problems and calamities had
poured in. They were like portable toilets at the end of a
particularly busy rock festival. The employees' faces showed
this too, and a corporate grimace covered them all today. There
were no smiles, no quips or attempts at jokes, no Friday
afternoon-style frivolities, nor were they expected either. There
was a rather depressing acceptance that the place, and their
lives, should feel like this. That, rather than bask in the glory of
a sunny day, wear little, feel the heat of the sun and welcome its
rays on your face, you should simply transport to the end of
November, wear more jumpers and cover your features with
the hood of your coat when the early snow gets too much to
bear.

And then *he* arrived, the baby, just twenty-one days old. That
little parcel of light brought in by his mother, her timing
deliberate, perhaps, to cheer them all up possibly. Suddenly the
train of grimness was halted for a while. The phones rang out
until they eventually stopped, desks were abandoned, and
emails were left half-written while their authors' attentions were
gratefully diverted.

They all gathered around him in the centre of the room,
gently tweaking his toes and rubbing his cheeks. It wasn't long
before all the last remnants of sternness were replaced by
smiles. They introduced a curious new language now that they
all used. It didn't consist of words, more of soft comforting
sounds, which seemed to be mysteriously understood by
everybody there.

Fiona was the last to join the group. She looked more
obligated than willing to integrate, as she left her desk and
ambled slowly over. She peered in from the outside of the circle
until rather intriguingly the baby tilted his head and looked
straight up at her. Fiona appeared taken aback at first and then
a little embarrassed as everyone turned to face her.

"Oh, he likes *you*," his mother said, and the group parted to allow this special guest through. Once in front of him, Fiona took his outstretched hand, and she smiled warmly.

"You're so beautiful, aren't you?" she said tenderly. The little child seized her finger with his other hand and wouldn't let it go. He looked deep into Fiona's eyes and held her there like a hypnotist does with their subject – frozen, guided and totally controlled as they reveal the contents of those dark, undiscovered rooms in their lives. After a while, the mother offered up her treasure to Fiona to hold, and this she did. Fiona remained there, locked in her cradling for as long as she could – until his mother somewhat forcefully wrenched her baby clear from her again.

"Are you *really* sure you want that?" Martin's words cut cruelly in, and broke Fiona from her moment. "That's a big commitment. You can't go screwing other people's lives up just because you think you should be doing something else." Martin furrowed his brow a little before he uttered his next words, as if he necessarily expected some pain from their passing. "I've not had kids," he continued, "because that's a danger I'm not ready to face yet – and mainly for their benefit."

Fiona grinned knowingly.

"And because no one wants to have any with you as well, possibly?"

Martin returned her gesture of relief.

"Yes, there is that small point too, I suppose. But there's more to life than being compliant, breeding and getting old."

As Martin prepared to continue speaking, something on one of the shelves in the kitchen took his eye. He broke away momentarily and walked over to it. He picked up the object and studied it with fondness. It was a cup, well-used, but also very pretty. It was heavily patterned with red roses, which were bright and happy-looking, bold and easy on the eye. This was

Rob's favourite cup, and it brought an instant joy to anyone who saw it. They'd always wondered about why he used it, and they found it a little amusing too. It was like discovering a little old lady mixed in with all that grunt and machismo. It suggested the cup and its saucer had been given to him, a gift perhaps, something precious, cherished and worth withstanding all the teasing for. Martin put it carefully and respectfully back down on the shelf again and turned back to Fiona.

"I really think I understand now why Rob tried for the record," he said, somewhat soulfully.

"What, his … *craving*, you mean?"

"It's really *not* that simple." Martin hesitated and addressed Fiona with more certainty now. "So what have *we* done, Fiona? What will we be remembered for? A lot of people will be remembered for doing something. A few people will be remembered for doing something *really* special, but as it stands, we will be remembered for jack shit let alone something brave."

"Now who's being simplistic?"

"But wouldn't you like to be?"

"Bravery doesn't equate to recklessness. My grandmother was brave, but she wasn't reckless."

"How do you know? Were you with her?"

Fiona's head lowered and she seemed unable to respond. It was as if Martin's prying question made her suddenly examine parts of this other person's life. Her expression now was one of confusion. She looked lost, as if she was trying to discover something that perhaps she could never find. She was fishing in a dead pond. She appeared weak and envious, as if she was guessing at definitions but not fully experiencing them. It was as if her grandmother was asking this question of her, not Martin, and she couldn't answer her — like an avid fan speaks out in defence of their pop star idol. That's the difference; the fan knows what a pop star is, their songs and music, what they've done; but they're not the star themselves and so they have no idea of what it's really like to be one. They ape, drool, wish; but never become.

Martin read Fiona's lack of a reply as 'no'. But he was kinder now. He seemed to realise she was sinking in a swamp, and with a more compassionate tone, he laid a plank down for her to make it back across.

"So?" Martin enquired carefully. "What did she do?"

"Why should I tell *you*?"

"Because you brought her up, cited her as evidence."

Fiona smiled with admiration a little as she recalled the memories of her grandmother. And then she winced slightly. But not because they were hazy, difficult to recount perhaps, but more because of what these memories contained, that it was so incredible these events happened at all; all that cruelty, all that bravery, those unsurmountable, tiny odds.

"She was in the war," Fiona carried on, "in a special unit, behind enemy lines. She was decorated afterwards – extensively."

"Wow!"

"She never told us much about it, but we knew it was life or death for her. We knew she risked absolutely everything and survived – but only just. Okay, she was brave, but she also had this … *balance* too." Fiona's face fell. "I miss her so terribly."

It was now evident that Martin was preparing to tell Fiona something difficult. He averted his eyes, indecision there, as if he was wrestling with whether to deliver his next words. Fiona picked up on the presence of this harbinger. But then Martin became more determined; a decision made. He connected forcefully with her gaze.

"I don't want that record – or Rob – just to be forgotten," he said doggedly, "to simply sink to the bottom of the Pit and be lost for ever. In truth, I don't think it'll let me do that either. I really *do* understand where Rob was coming from, and that's why ... that's why I'm going to film it, get it teched-out properly, documented; recorded ..."

Fiona glared at him.

"... You're attempting it yourself!" she gasped with incredulity. "After all we've just talked about, after all that's happened? Now you're just into lunacy."

Martin responded to her criticism by looking sheepish.

"It gets worse, I'm afraid," he said smirking.

"How can it possibly get worse?"

He grinned and waited a few seconds before replying.

"Because ... I want you to buddy with me on it."

"Very funny."

Then Fiona realised he was serious and she wrenched herself away in disgust. There was a highly awkward pause.

"What would your grandmother say?" Martin probed, finally breaking in. Fiona swung back to face him, anger now in her eyes.

"She hardly ever swore," she retorted, "but in your case, I think she'd make a significant exception. The answer's no, Martin, and come on – it should be for you too!"

Martin stood tall.

"So when did you lose your fighting spirit?" he demanded. "When did you piss on that fire in your belly?"

Fiona took a pace towards him fearlessly.

"Rob's just died trying this damned thing you all want to do so badly!" she shouted. "That's not a story in a book, some TV soap episode, a video game; it's fact. Rob's dead, gone; never to return – just like a whole bunch of other people. Whatever convinced you to think I would ever try that dive with you!"

"Are you a virgin, Fiona?"

"What?"

"Are you?"

"Of course I'm not. What kind of dumb-ass question is that to ask anyone?"

"Because the principle's the same, what are you saving yourself for, exactly? You got all teary-eyed about children before. But what excuses do we have for not trying something that's off-the-scale mad? Because if you were telling me you didn't want to try something risky because of your kids, then I'd possibly understand. But as we don't have any then in one sense that makes things even worse for us, doesn't it?"

"And so how does that work then?"

"Have you ever thought that outside work, diving is all we have? Take that away and the feeble floods in. In one way, childless couples are some of the bravest people around. They're fully exposed; there's no excuses about their children's welfare for them to hide behind. But you're thinking about quitting diving for the precise reason of … nothing. If I've become obsessed with that record, then you've become obsessed with the mundane. And soon after you change, give it all up, you'll become imprisoned by your own bitterness, corrupted; ruined by it."

Then Martin was quiet for a moment. He allowed the situation to settle, the way a nearly-discovered fish lets the ripples calm before moving on again. He found a chair and sat before speaking once more.

"There's this man who comes in our gym …"

Fiona lunged forwards suddenly, pointing.

"… Why should I listen to your shit – do you think!"

Martin reached out and lowered her finger gently with his hand.

"Because you need to?" he answered softly.

Fiona reluctantly moved back.

"God."

She sat again now too, almost as if she was expecting agony and needed support. Martin swivelled slightly on his chair, finding more space in which to express himself.

"He's one of *them*," he began, "*transformed*." Martin's face tightened suddenly with anger. "Fifties, minute, so thin he almost disappears." He took a moment to relish the image. "It'd be easy to pity him – but you shouldn't. Not that someone's size matters one bit. Generally, everyone who goes in there is a nice person. We're all sharing in the pain, trying for a personal best, keeping healthy; fighting back the years. But this little shit eyeballs everyone. It's decidedly odd. We all catch someone's eye occasionally, and they respond: 'All right? How's it going?' 'Good, thanks. You?' 'Feel better in an hour's time, eh?' And we laugh, enjoying the humour, but him; deliberately straight in on the confrontation. But none of us respond, of course. Who wants to be in court for GBH – or worse? But that's the card he's playing, isn't it; sheltering under the umbrella of some misplaced justice? It's the very worst kind of cowardice. And he's no Ninja either. I've fought against small, dangerous people in competitions and he's not one of those. In my experience, as well as being deadly, they're perfectly delightful people. They've earned their respect, and they're content. They have that privilege."

Martin looked directly at Fiona to see if she was paying attention. He looked almost surprised to discover that she was.

"And when you *do* look back at this man," he continued, "return the confrontation; he quickly averts his eyes. But sooner or later you'll feel them on you again as you carry on through your routine; it's so really, *really* tiresome. I don't know; maybe he's getting off on us all somehow. Flying around like some horrible little insect, settling on us, gathering nectar to store in his hive, in his wank bank for later on."

Martin smiled slightly. "Of course, millions of people use that tactic too, and not just in gyms. You and I see it every working day of our lives. We both deal with *that* woman at the council, don't we? Mealy-mouthed, devious, smug git with no

sense of humour and no balls. The way she operates; she's
doing exactly the same thing as our weirdo in the gym."

Martin stood and moved next to Fiona, looking down at her.

"But I don't want that epitome of ineptitude," he stated.
Fiona moved away a little, reclaiming her comfort zone. "I want
respect for myself by trying something daring – and I think you
do too." He paused as he looked deep into her eyes. "You
don't *really* want to leave the club, do you?" She didn't answer;
rather she looked away again. "Place me in a different pile,"
Martin resumed, but now more forcefully. "Don't put us in that
same category, hide us under that umbrella. Don't turn us into
bony, masturbating members of Total Fitness. Don't make us
mediocre like the rest of them." He hesitated. "Do you
understand what I mean?" he asked piercingly. Fiona didn't
reply, but she seemed unable to resist the point in his words.
Slowly she turned and faced him once more, and then looked
directly at him, holding her gaze for a while. Her initial
expression of objection, present only a few minutes before, was
replaced by one of deep and serious contemplation.

CHAPTER SIX

Their two lives were more alike than they might have first imagined, because Martin and Fiona had similar jobs; they both dealt with people. They might have been in different locations, but both their employers performed the same basic operations – they processed people, or more accurately, the issues they created. There was an odd kind of cycle working here with the difficulty of the problems matching the difficulty of the people, notch for notch. As the bar went higher, and the most challenging problems were reached, Martin and Fiona, as last resort practitioners, had to deal with the most challenging people.

Martin's office was barely a mile or so across the city centre from Fiona's. His building was much newer, however. Made mainly of concrete, it imitated buildings from the 1960s, when some joker thought big, grey, blocks of the stuff peppered with bland, tinny windows actually looked good. The large interior was square. There were shiny, matching desks and chairs, swish IT and comms too. But the layout hadn't been thought out terribly well, and in the open-plan space, danger lived. Conversations could be easily overheard, and office rumours and their resultant conflicts grew and then multiplied and festered like some rogue, rampant plague that contaminated everything.

Martin sat in a team of five, and he was working down his list of troublesome tenants. They'd try to talk first, and then all sorts of letters and court orders would follow if this failed. They were the country's largest social housing landlord. They painted pictures about their size and importance on their website, with examples showing how far the line of houses they owned would stretch if they were lined up side by side. This didn't seem to alter the behaviour of some of the tenants, however. They appeared to do whatever they wanted, whether the line was an inch or several thousand miles long.

Martin's building was cold too. There was a long-running dispute over what was the right working temperature, and the person who owned the code to the aircon controller liked it rather chilly. In winter especially, all the staff except one would turn into Eskimos, padded out, looking half their size again in their battle against the icy blasts coming from the weather outside and the freezing, abominable atmosphere from the office on the inside.

Fiona was in mid-flow by now. It was eleven o'clock in the morning and things were speeding up. All the staff here were given lists to work down too, and she'd had a bad morning so far. Her stats were down – or so she'd be reminded later. They were called 'consultants' nowadays, but Fiona moaned to her friends that she was still just a debt collector to everyone else.

Her office was laid out as a call-centre with rows of plastic, heartless, grey cubicles filling the floor. There were forty people crammed up on the second storey of the old, long-since bankrupted carpet mega-store with its awful address and consequential manageable rent. But then the owners of the business would need all the money they could muster. Debtors were better protected in today's climate with changes in the law – they needed to be talked down off ledges, gently, cautiously.

Gone were the days of simply shooting people with some hefty legislation and scraping them off the pavement.

From their little hutches, the staff were required to phone the company's clients to try to make contact. If, remarkably, they did, then they'd attempt to chase up the missed payments and possibly arrange a plan. Fiona was on the team that got the stodge. These were the really wearisome cases. These people were always well-armed with excuses, abuse and threats. But the management saw it as a failure if any of the consultants ditched the call simply because things were getting too rough. Of course, any normal person would have killed these calls off well before, but not here at Apex Services where 'solutions are our business'.

After the first two ring-outs, Fiona was about to give up on this particular client and move down her list. This *was* allowed. She couldn't force people to answer their phones after all; she didn't possess those kinds of powers. So, it surprised her greatly that just at the very last moment a voice came on the line. Now Fiona could begin.

Across town, Martin was having a comparable morning to Fiona, with some of his far from model tenants giving him grief. He was a housing officer, and his job could be very stressful and unrewarding. Police officers and bailiffs probably have the same problem. He managed a certain patch of this vast estate of 6,500 houses, which certainly had its share of troubles. To be fair, there were lots of decent, pleasant people living there, but the area also offered an impressive, multi-layered selection box of social deprivation.

Among the population were also people who simply couldn't be bothered to live nicely at all. They were a rare breed to be sure, but they existed all the same. Anyone in any kind of position of authority was automatically an enemy to them, and this conspiracy theory mentality seemed to give these tenants a kind of self-proclaimed right to be as awkward as they possibly could be in any situation they found themselves in. This included keeping the houses they rented in reasonable condition. Some of them almost literally lived like pigs, and it was the job of the housing officers to correct this behaviour. It could be a near-impossible task.

The voice on the other end of Fiona's line was feeble at first as if it was exploring, checking who was there. The accent sounded almost affected, put on, as if whoever was speaking was trying to conceal their true identity. Fiona soon engaged with them though. She found that using her first name worked best – and throwing in a question.

"Hi, this is Fiona from Apex. How are you today?" Then as she talked more, gave the reason for her call, the tone in the returning voice changed. It was duller, less enthusiastic, less camouflaged and there were longer silences between her questions.

"Don't worry, I won't keep you long," seemed to help and the inflexion in her doom-ridden line: "It might be better if we talked," rather surprisingly seemed to capture him. Soon she was discussing details, exploring options; seeing what could be done.

Martin wasn't so fortunate, however. His attempts at connecting were going nowhere. He could hear the television on in the background. It was one of those strange reality TV shows; strange because somehow millions of people so easily empathise with other people's remote lives when their own are in tatters – and they seem entirely happy to leave things that way.

"Would you mind turning that off?" Martin eventually requested. There was a grumbling noise, which sounded like a heavy lorry passing, and then the TV went silent. "Good," Martin said and tried again. "Thank you."

He pushed his stalked microphone closer to his mouth as
the information on his client rolled down the screen in front of
him. Martin's expression told his on-looking colleagues that this
was going to be a ball-ache of a call. Ten minutes later and
Martin was still at the same place in their conversation.

"With respect, Mrs McDonnell," Martin continued, "we *are*
being reasonable." The constant interruptions and cuttings-in
from his caller had turned what should have been a three-
minute talk into where they were now. "We're simply asking
you to stop your dog fouling at our property," Martin persisted
and then hastily lifted one side of his headset away from his ear
as a stream of amplified abuse flooded out through it. "Please,
can you let me finish?"

Fiona's caller seemed to be running out of steam; if cooperation
was gas under a kettle, then the knob on the cooker was
suddenly turned down low.

"With respect, Mr Price," she insisted down her mic, "we *are*
being fair. You haven't paid us for six months now, and we've
constantly had to chase you."

She couldn't have known it, but she mimicked Martin's
reaction to the abuse she now received almost identically, only
she held her headset marginally further away from her ear as the
expletives hurried down the wire. "Please, can you let me
finish?"

"After our housing officer visited," Martin resumed doggedly,
"they logged it as a serious danger to health — and you have
young children there, do you not, Mrs McDonnell?" And then
the interruption again. "Can you *please* let me finish."
Unsurprisingly, their conversation was halted abruptly again as
more abuse followed.

"That's not correct, Mr Price," Fiona persevered with her caller. "You've ignored all our letters and all our phone calls. We've had no response from you in the last twenty-six weeks … Can you *please* let me finish?" And now, like Martin, she was stuck in a traffic jam of invectives once again.

"You are a tenant in our property," Martin carried on, "And you're not just letting your dog foul *at* our property, you're letting your dog foul *in* our property; in the lounge to be exact, and for several months now by the looks of things – and you own a Great Dane." Now Martin ripped the headset from his head as the foul language intensified. It was as if he'd suddenly discovered a scorpion wriggling in his earpiece.

"We really *have* been fair." Fiona set off again. Everyone around her could see that she was trying to maintain her composure, but also that this was failing her. Here was that moment with a pie in the oven when the gravy starts to seep through the edges of the crust after thirty-five minutes on two hundred degrees. Volumes are expanding and their consequences evident.

"Your credit card debt with us stands at just over fourteen thousand pounds," she went on. "Our agreed repayment plan is ten pounds a month. At that rate it'll be twenty-one-thirty-four when the debt is repaid – and you will one hundred and sixty-three."

Across town, another scorpion scurried from the safety of its home and explored new ground. And in her reaction to remove her headset, Fiona accidentally knocked over her glass of water that had been standing on her desk. Trapped by her situation, she could do nothing to stem it or clean it up, save create a safe channel for it to flow down. It crept along in a tiny river and then fell unceremoniously on to the floor. She watched it for a moment as it carried on its way. Her expression changed. She looked immediately depressed, as if the water now represented the life that was being drained from her daily, hourly, minute-by-minute by her tedious, remarkably disheartening job. Her veins let, the smell of iron out now, goodness and nutrients so easily squandered by the monotony of these people she was forced to engage with so relentlessly. The water was now her own blood and, in a way, envied, because at least the life of the water was being expended as its drips splattered on to the well-worn vinyl by her feet. Could she have been relieved from her torment so effortlessly? One simple, swift cut would suffice. It would all be over so easily.

"Now you're swearing at me, Mrs McDonnell," Martin protested to his caller, the receiver back on his ear but a hand poised ready to wrench it clear again.

"You're swearing at me, Mr Price," Fiona protested too.

And now Martin's and her actions were unwittingly intertwined, like dancers treading the same floor, their waltz superbly coordinated but distanced at the same time.

"I …" Martin began but was cut off again.

"I …" Fiona tried too but met a similar blockage.

"No …"

"No …"

"Please stop swearing, Mrs McDonnell."

"Will you please stop swearing, Mr Price."

"If you threaten me again, I will terminate the call."

"If you threaten me again, I will have to end the call."

"I …" Martin tried once more.

"You …" Fiona too.

"You …"

"I …"

"Mrs …"

"Mr …"

"Stop threatening me, Mrs McDonnell," Martin tried for a final time.

"Will you stop threatening me, Mr Price."

As the last of the water dribbled on to the floor from her desk, Fiona pulled her headset clear from its perch on her skull and looked at it as if it was a physical part of her caller. Down the road, Martin copied her action. Then, almost at the same time, they uttered exactly the same words:

"Fuck this!" they exclaimed.

Martin's headset hit the desk first; hard and noisy. Fiona's followed closely after, startling most of the room who were now looking on. Then:

"Wanker!" they both shouted out deafeningly together.

CHAPTER SEVEN

The howls of the dogs were what they heard next. First, there'd
been the shouts. They'd come from a group of ten or so men.
They were casual shouts at first. They'd been a mixture of
operational instructions and false observations. And then they
changed. Now, these shouts became high-pitched, excited,
grateful almost; suggesting that those issuing them had finally
found something tangible that pleased them. And they had. The
hounds had picked up scents, engaged with them and locked
on.

The two men running ahead of the group suddenly stopped.

"Fuck," Rob hissed.

"So, what now?" the man with him asked, fear flowing
readily through his voice. Rob looked around, speaking softly as
he did so.

"Give me a moment," he replied calmly, as his eyes ripped
into the scenery around them, dissecting everything, looking for
a way out; a chance to escape. But then the howls and the
voices got louder, and then came that one dreadful, single, little
word that confirmed they'd been discovered.

One of the lead dogs halted the pack and sniffed the ground
close by assuredly. Then a command from one of the soldiers,
and all the men began to cluster around a particular spot,
narrowing in from their fanned-out formation, bounding and
weaving through the forest, now looking like a pack of hounds
themselves. Rob crouched down low, and the other man copied

him. Quickly, Rob's eyes settled on something fifty metres away, and he looked considerately to the comrade by his side.

"Do you remember that exercise we did in training with the reeds?" he enquired rather than asked, still sounding incredibly composed. "You know; the one you hated so much?"

"Aw, shit."

Rob smiled.

"It's that, or we're royally fucked, mate," he said.

They'd been in tight situations before, but nothing quite like this. What had started out as a high-risk, basic recon mission had now turned into something significantly more perilous. But then again, you wouldn't normally find yourself in a location like this. This wasn't a holiday destination. There were no tour guides to show you around, no nice hotels, golden beaches, all-inclusive luxuries to indulge in. This was light years away from all that gushing hospitality. If entering some of the most restricted territory on earth, where you could be shot on sight, counted as a vacation, then certainly Rob and his accomplice had bagged this six-star palace easily enough; their initials embroidered on the towels by the pool, private waiting-on staff provided – everything.

They were just over the border in North Korea, south of Kaesong. Tensions with the West, and especially certain parts of it, were getting high again. It was like observing a relationship between a drug addict on rehab and those treating them. There'd be ups and downs, falling-ons and falling-offs, with damaging consequences for both sides. This was a period when the programme was definitely failing everyone, and so other more desperate measures had to be hurriedly put in place.

There were rumours that a new nuclear facility had recently been built. A closer look had been deemed 'critically essential', and that's what Rob and his companion had been assigned to do. They'd crept in and collected their evidence; just before they'd been exposed and had found it necessary to flee for their lives, that is. Their first shots had missed, but now the soldiers were hot on their heels with the promise of more. They'd cleared some good ground, but now Rob and his comrade were trailing behind in this frantic race for survival.

Rob suddenly led them off at a ninety-degree tangent. Now they were running perpendicular to their pursuers. It was a risky manoeuvre given how visible they could ultimately be, but Rob's determination implied he knew what he was doing. Soon they reached a pond some forty metres across, filled with gloomy, deep water, topped by a variety of thickly embedded water lilies and edged by reeds. It was a place you could easily have imagined snakes and alligators living in.

Without stopping, Rob waded straight into the water until he was standing knee-high in the thick, all-consuming mud. It sucked at his feet and contained him like an over-possessive lover. His companion joined him and, uttering no words, Rob bent down and picked a reed from down by his side, bit off both ends and rounded its stem. He held it horizontally and then placed one end in his mouth. He pointed to the other end indicating that the man with him should copy his action. He did so and there they were, locked, held in a balance where their breath was the same, linked by the reed. Neither of them moved. It was if they were recalling a skill they'd learned a long time ago but hadn't recently used.

Pinching their noses, they took no outer air but relied solely on the combined breath contained within their lungs to sustain them, passing it between them in a to and fro of even inhalations and exhalations. As they did this, they walked slowly into the water side by side until they were submerged. Once under the surface, they descended further into the middle of the pond, following the terrain of its bottom. They took care to minimise the disturbance of the silt, and after a few more paces, they sat quietly on its bed.

The advancing soldiers initially passed them by, and looking up through the haze of the water, Rob and his accomplice saw them clear the pond. But then the leading soldier suddenly stopped. It was as if an instinct or hunch took over him and he shouted out an order to the group behind him. His flailing arms spun them out in a search of the immediate area. Slowly, little by little, with all other nearby ground exhausted and devoid of bounty, the group congregated around this patch of water. Now all their eyes were directed down through the surface, scouring, piercing; looking for life.

A shrill shout suddenly rang out followed by a pointing hand. Something under the water over by the far bank took this soldier's eye, and he discharged a wild volley of shots from his assault rifle. Some of the others followed, blasting the mud and killing the few fish that were basking there. As their bodies rose to the surface, the laugh of the soldier sounded out; followed by the bludgeoning remonstration from his commanding officer. *He* then scanned the pond for one more time and then ordered the majority of his men away, off back into the forest. He left two soldiers by the bank however, as if for a contingency. Now Rob and his comrade could see the soldiers looking into the depths like predatory pike lurking in the shadows.

Rob touched his companion's shoulder gently, reassuringly, and then he made an 'OK' sign with his hand to ask if he was all right. His companion returned the gesture signifying that he was. They'd both need to be well too because it was here where the terror could begin. Eventually their shared air would become stale, the oxygen would be totally depleted, and they would be vulnerable. They'd been in this state for seven minutes already, and there would be all sorts of natural urges they would have to fight against and control. The desire to race to the surface to breathe would be damn near irresistible, but they had to maintain their composure. Any sudden move now, any ripple of any kind would give them away, and death would almost certainly follow. Believing that the plastic bag that's been thrust over your head and then tightened at its base will eventually be removed and you'll be free to breathe again: this is a call which is almost beyond faith.

The two North Korean soldiers remained still for a while, then they began another sweep of the pond, pacing its circumference in opposite directions. When they met halfway round, they gave the water one last final, thorough examination. Up through the surface, Rob met one of their stares head on and the soldier lingered on their bizarre exchange. Perhaps realising that any change in light or reflection could attract suspicion, Rob kept his eyes open, and the dirty water began to sting. Twenty seconds later, thankfully, the solider looked away again. He concentrated his attention on the radio that he withdrew from inside his uniform. A few words spoken into it, a command received, and then the two soldiers moved from their spot and went on their way.

Rob and his comrade remained underwater for another ninety seconds. Because of the time they had spent there, the fish had started to become accustomed to their company, and they floated happily around their heads. The two men looked as if they were wearing odd, naturally assembled crowns, which rapidly dissipated as the two men slowly moved.

They broke the surface of the pond together, carefully and only partially, like the rising snouts of hippos, the creatures returning from a spell on the bottom of a riverbed somewhere. Still in complete silence, the two men scanned the vicinity and, satisfied that their enemies were gone, they swam to the edge of the pond. Rob quickly fixed a bearing on the compass on his wrist, and pointing in the opposite direction to where the soldiers had exited, they set off. By nightfall, they were back at the South Korean border. By midnight, they were safely secured in the agent's house. A good bath, and then they all shared a beautifully cold beer together – and their priceless intel.

One of the five unknown visitors was still fixated on the tube of children's straws that had been left on one of the tables by the catering company. Rob's funeral had been a success, if such a thing was possible. People had paid their respects, made speeches and said their goodbyes; but these five men had been silent throughout the proceedings, keeping themselves to themselves, even here at the subsequent reception. They were all young. None of them was over the age of thirty, and they all looked incredibly fit. They also looked incredibly sad. Despite this, there was a razor-sharp alertness to them, and they caught every movement. Even now as they sat in a group, it was noticeable how they seemed to have every angle around them covered. It was obvious to the accustomed eye that they must have worked extensively as a team, watching backs and covering danger.

Over on one of the corporate-looking sofas in this modern hotel, a couple of women were sitting. They were distant relatives, judging by their accumulating boredom; no doubt wrenched there by some cousin or other, herded to the event by obligation. They'd eaten their free sandwiches and bravely taken two full glasses of Merlot each. Now they were entertaining themselves by searching around the room for people to pick on. They'd whisper to each other, identify their next victim, make a remark and giggle. They'd been sussing out the man looking at the straws for some time now. He must have seemed like a perfect target. He was detached, oblivious; an easy kill. The taller woman's eyes settled on him, and a cynical, cruel smile began to creep over her face like suffocating ivy.

"God," she croaked mercilessly. "Look at that sad wanker getting all grossed-out over a bunch of kids' fucking straws!"

In a flash, the man staring at the straws moved his gaze directly to the two women who were now grinning. The compassion, admiration and love in his eyes were replaced in an instant by hate, threat and a tangible intention to inflict pain. As he transferred his attention, the other four men with him did the same. Now they were a common band of menace and destruction with one clear aim. The taller woman's grin vaporised, and she gulped as their eyes connected with her. She swiftly pivoted her head to face her accomplice next to her, as if begging for help, turning rapidly pale as she did so. The women looked at each other helplessly, and they seemed paralysed, not sure what to do; unexpectedly petrified.

CHAPTER EIGHT

Martin had aged disproportionately since Rob's death; a couple of months had now accelerated into years. There were odd, grey shoots of hair sprouting by his temples, making him look older than he was. Sometimes this can be flattering, giving the impression of wisdom, but in this instance, Martin simply looked jaded. He'd not been sleeping as well as he could either, and this was evident by the condition of the skin on his face. It looked tired and worn now, like a pair of well-used gardening shoes, their material stretched and distorted by all the strain and effort from countless days of tending.

Tonight, he sat in the far end of the lounge in his house, and he appeared comfortable there; cocooned and safe. The dwelling was a semi-detached, built in the 1950s and, like him, it too was beginning to show its age. Its windows were weathered, the original plain pine doors were unchanged, and several tiles were missing from its roof. It was pretty much paid for, however, so perhaps the humiliation Martin endured by being behind in housing fashion stakes was amply compensated for by the lack of worry about money.

The house had three average-sized bedrooms, a bathroom, a small kitchen and this walk-through lounge, which doubled as a dining area. He had an old lady as a neighbour. She was now so hard of hearing that Martin could pick up almost every word on her ridiculously turned-up TV. He'd use this to his advantage, however, and in serious moments of indulgence, he'd rack up the volume of his rock music to match her every decibel.

As compact as the house was, two of its bedrooms remained unused. They were left, part-cluttered with furniture that hardly ever saw a face and gathered dust. The tatty garden was around twenty metres long, and it overlooked a broad spread of fields. To one side there was a rather odd-looking hawthorn tree, which was stumpy due to the battering it received from the prevailing winds. The lawn, such as it was, was tufted due to lack of care.

To the side of this though was a broad section of bare earth that had been meticulously tilled, and by its side, a new medium-sized greenhouse had been erected, its windows scrubbed and polished to perfection. Inside, there was neatly positioned wooden staging, on which stood an assortment of trays and plant pots.

The lounge was cosy and decorated with bold, red colours. The curtains were designer, high-end and expensive, matching the thick, luxuriant carpets. The lampshade hanging from the ceiling was ornate too, comprising hand-crafted, shaded glass which distributed a comforting glow. There were subtle copies of period portraits hung on the walls, and the whole room emitted a feeling of refuge.

In the dining area of the lounge where Martin sat, a different décor took over, and it was here where things changed in quality more than a little. It was as if the entire room had been gifted with a budget, but it was at this point where the boundary of opulence ended, where the poor relative resided.

Martin sat by the circular, functional dining table that he'd bought from the local cheap furniture store. Its imitation oak veneer was dinted and marked in places, but there'd been no effort made to cover these with a table cloth or other embellishments. It had a stark honesty about it. He was perched underneath the dish-shaped, rather-too-bright light which hung from the ceiling on its raw, white flex. It was set a little too low, and there were a couple of indentations which ruined its once perfect shape; blows from a head perhaps, or some act of violent revenge justly served out after receiving them.

Martin took a swig from his bottle of Becks, taking care not to spill any of it as he did so. He found his well-beaten pub beer mat again and set the bottle down. Then he looked at the piece of paper positioned on the table in front of him.

"Come on then," he mumbled aloud, "let's get this over with."

The sheet of paper was a letter with irregular lines of handwritten text extending down to its lower edge. A ballpoint pen was placed by the side of it, but at such a distance away that it looked like a decision had been taken not to use it again. It seemed to suggest that the letter was a final and finished version and no additions or amendments could be made before it was sent on its way.

Another long, extended swig of his Becks, and Martin picked up the letter and readied it for reading. He studied it briefly. He wore a tinge of bitterness on his face, and he held the letter as if it was a witness statement or testimony. He cleared his throat and then began reading it aloud.

"I've addressed this to both of you because I turned forty today" – he looked up and away from the page for a moment, suddenly sad and angry – "and it's made me think." Then he paused and sighed, almost as if he was picturing something in his head, some past conflict perhaps. Then he resumed his reading again.

"Maybe it's time to try and put things right between us. Maybe it's time to look at things from a completely different perspective, from a unique point of view; fresh." He smiled, pondering this quandary. "Like what it smells like in space," he carried on again. "Diesel fumes, barbeques and gunpowder, apparently. The aroma's mostly produced by dying stars, so they say. How the hell do I find these things? And I know I'm rambling on, but the point is, time's racing by. That's the truth of it, isn't it? I've been planning my garden for the summer this week, and that's made me think too."

Martin looked content now. There was another picture in his head, but a more congenial one this time, judging by the warm expression he wore.

"Everything else is sorted." He took care with his next words. "Tomatoes, onions, potatoes; and then I came across the choice of lettuces. Boring stuff, I know. But you can have leaves or hearts; that's the drill. I normally have leaves. You keep the plant in the ground and take two leaves from the outside when you need them, and then they grow back again. Thing is, though ..." He glanced away from the page, and his meandering text, quickly, and settled on an old photograph of himself on the mantelpiece, taken many years before. He looked athletic, handsome; happy. Then back to the page again. "I've realised today that my leaves won't keep growing back for ever, will they? – and that my season is coming to an end." His voice was slower now; more sincere.

"*Will* you consider meeting up? See if we can sort all this out? Be nice if we could."

He paused, and then dropped his line of sight from the letter again. "Sort all this out," he mused rhetorically. "No." He shook his head, and suddenly any warmth in his voice was gone. "You never will, will you?" he snarled, "Or you would have done it by now. You don't want to. It's just *dead*; isn't it?" He became emotional, almost as if he was digesting his own words, listening to them in detail, now fully understanding the implications of their true meaning. A tear came, and he wiped it away from his eye with the back of his wrist. Then the anger returned. "You'll never change, no matter what space or lettuces bring. You'll just be the same." He scanned around the room looking for something that clearly wasn't there. "Christ –

63

and a card would have been nice," he scorned cuttingly, and he screwed up the letter into a tight, compact little ball. "What's the point?" he scoffed, and hurled it all the way down to the other end of the room. After he watched it land, roll and then become stationary, he spoke for one last time. "Fuck it. I'll just 'not bother' too," he said.

CHAPTER NINE

The mid evenings were the worst times for Fiona. The chaos of getting home and making her dinner served as a handy diversion, as did the encroaching fatigue of the later hours, but now, once she'd settled down, meal in hand, TV turned prematurely off, as she'd become bored and irritated by it again; now was the most dangerous period. Things could land now. They would descend from the atmosphere like one of those deceptive, fine mists that saturates everything.

She'd felt it coming, and so she'd taken shelter; albeit in the comfort of her own flat. She'd fought against it so well for the last three hours, but now it had consumed her, and in a desperate attempt to escape it, she'd hobbled through to her bedroom. Under the bed covers seemed to be the safest place for her to go, and there she'd hidden; a thin, cotton, pristine sheet like a fortress wall for her now, keeping the intruders out, well, for a little while at least. And then her tears came as her anguish intensified.

"If you're truly there for me like you used to be," she pleaded through the fabric and into the space of the room beyond, "help me, please. I have no one. I feel so alone."

She became a little bolder now, and she squirmed up the bed to clear the covers. She wrapped her hands around her head, as if she'd just suffered some real physical injury. But still her eyes were averted as if there was something there in the room with her. She avoided any contact, the way people do with savage animals; willingly allowing them their territory and avoiding deadly fights.

"It's all around me," she spoke out again, addressing this invisibility. "It's getting stronger every day. Everything I've done to try and fight it isn't working."

She looked skywards now and found the small but pretty lampshade in the centre of the room with its mock-chandeliered look which mirrored her flat – expensive, possibly overrated, and somewhat pretentious.

"I thought I was strong," she continued, "that I could defeat; conquer anything. But this is something I never saw coming, not in my wildest dreams. It's like, I'm looking into the shadows and it's there, staring right back at me; a satisfied smile already on its cruel, formidable face." She looked despairingly out into the middle of the room. "What the hell am I going to do?"

Fiona waited for an answer, which she seemed to know was perhaps never going to come. And then the full force of her terror bore down on her again, like the way a returning fever recaptures people; gone for a while so they feel stronger, and so they move. They try their limbs again, feel brighter momentarily, but then they sense the return of the aches, the sickness, the burning brow and so slowly and depressingly, they succumb to its influence once more; they deteriorate; fall back.

Fiona felt for the secure, inviting mattress, and without looking down, she settled eagerly back into her former position. She began to cry, bitterly, and then slowly she pulled the sheet back over her and gratefully hid in her fragile, safe cave once again.

CHAPTER TEN

"Is there anything planned for next Monday?" Martin had asked Fiona as they'd left the clubhouse on the preceding Sunday evening. She'd obviously found this an odd question when he'd asked it at the time, and this was reflected in her response.

"No, it'll be empty. It *is* a Monday, Martin. Most of us are back at work, remember?"

She'd largely dismissed his enquiry at the time, but it had left a niggle in her head like a lively maggot that wouldn't stop wriggling. Later on, his question would make perfect sense and thankfully it would motivate her to act.

The Monday in question had arrived. Martin pulled up in his slightly-too-old-to-look-that-cool Mitsubishi L200 Warrior utility truck. He was on his own, and there was no one else around. Fiona's prediction was correct, and Martin appeared more than a little relieved when he realised this was the case. He fumbled for his set of keys to the building and let himself in. He closed the door quickly behind him and left the rather grim late-autumn day on the other side of the thick wood. It felt like an anxious, troublesome sort of day and it matched the stress etched deep into Martin's face.

Once inside, he found a space on the floor for the holdall he was carrying and made himself a cup of tea. Then he sat on one of the sofas for a while. Time seemed to be of the essence to him as he checked his watch at regular intervals. But it was as if he needed this break as a moment of contemplation, as if he'd finally decided something; committed to it, even.

When he finished his tea, he studied the empty cup, and he smiled affectionately at it before standing, moving to the sink, washing it carefully and then gently placing it back on the shelf in its rightful place once more. Martin moved the handle of the rose-patterned china inwards away from the danger of glancing, passing elbows and wafting, expression-driven arms so it wouldn't be harmed in any way. With one last, fleeting glance he picked up his holdall and moved over to a table which sat in the far corner of the room, and which had the best view over the waters of the Pit.

The first thing he looked for was a plug socket. He spotted one that was free and uncluttered. Seeing this, Martin began unloading the contents of his bag. He looked like a magician, drawing out things that shouldn't reasonably have been accommodated in it. He concluded with a laptop, which he positioned strategically in the middle of the table and turned so its screen faced inwards to the room and the handy chair he'd set there before it.

The screen sparked to life and soon a rather technical-looking programme loaded, which displayed various graphs and dials. The main one was a depth gauge, which had a scale in both metres and feet calibrated on it. In one of the USB ports, there was a dongle which flashed very importantly. Martin took out a wristband, which housed a large, clear dial. This had a read-out too. He switched it on, and there was a bleep. After two seconds, it was evident that the reading on the wrist-mounted device matched that on the dial on the laptop screen. They both read '+0.45m'.

Happy that all the equipment was functioning correctly, Martin left it running and wandered outside to the small beach that bordered the lake. He looked out over the water as if he was inspecting, checking for things; boats, people or hazards

there; conducting some kind of drill. His line of sight went next
to the surface of the water. He looked like the captain of a ship
in the Second World War examining his plotted course for the
possibility of enemy U-boats skulking under the waves. Then,
appearing satisfied with his findings, he looked up to the sky
momentarily. There was a flock of Canada geese flying
overhead, and he watched them for a while. He wore a
temporary expression of envy on his face as he studied them in
free-flight, going on their way. When they disappeared into the
far distance, he stood straight and then spoke confidently to
himself:

"Come on then, mate," he said, and walked determinedly
back towards the clubhouse. A strong push on the door and he
was back inside.

The water had taken no time in losing its heat. The remnants
of the Indian summer had passed two weeks ago now, but had
failed to sustain the temperatures of the more pleasant previous
months. Things were relatively comfortable topside, but down
here at twenty metres it was significantly chillier.

The sunlight was fading too, and the tails of its more
obstinate shafts passed by Martin like phantom lances as he
waited, weaving slightly – side to side and up and down – as he
peered down into the depths of the Incident Pit below his feet.
There was little sound, save the tinkle of his exhaled air, which
rippled to the surface like strings of tiny ribbons. The darkness
beneath him oozed out feelings of isolation, loneliness,
foreboding and dread. Martin looked upwards for one last time,
and then he spoke into the microphone embedded in his
facemask.

"God, this is amazing," he exclaimed, sounding both
overwhelmed and enthusiastic at the same time. And then more
stable and balanced: "I hope this is coming through to you guys
up there. I wanted to keep a record, just in case I make it down.
My camera's rolling too. Hopefully, you'll have a read-out on

the depths as well so I can substantiate all this, prove that I'm not just sat in the pub with a lovely pint of Bavarian lager enjoying myself, inventing everything."

He gazed out into the distance.

"I can see the first of the pylons." His eyes picked out something massive. "There's a huge earth mover just … left. It's like a whole new world down here." And then that more serious tone, resigned almost: "It's been twenty-five minutes now," he went on. "I need to watch the air."

And there he stayed for a while, engrossed, awestruck by the wonder of it all, appearing so vulnerable. The small group of fish that had gathered by his side flittered and danced around him as if they were inspecting, examining things too; as if they were asking what he was doing down there, why he was present in this hostile, alien world at all. But of course, he'd done his best to explain that on a previous occasion.

"There's been a lot of speculation, rumours and *comment* about what I'm going to do, so rather than let these run out of control and fester and rot like a two-week-old ham salad sandwich in a grubby lunch box, I thought I'd tell everyone the real facts myself; hence" – Martin looked around the room quickly – "this."

He stood in front of the group of twenty or so who were assembled in the adequate but rather shabby meeting room he'd hired at the local hotel.

"I've never held a 'press conference' before," Martin continued and grinned. "It's all rather grand, isn't it? I thought only celebrities did these kinds of things when they've found a new pimple on their arse or something. Anyway, thank you all very much for coming today."

There were a variety of journalists in the room; no TV though – he'd not managed to get them despite his persistence over the last week. When he'd been on the phone to the stations – to those who he could get through to, that is – he'd joked about how he'd be like an annoying gnat that wouldn't leave them alone. He'd told them he'd keep buzzing them until they agreed to come. It hadn't worked, sadly, but there were enough representatives of the media here today to get his message more than adequately across.

Martin paced left to right and back, assembling his words before he began speaking again.

"The Incident Pit: you've probably heard about that place already," he resumed. "Some of you carried quite a bit on it after Rob died. The physical aspects are easy to explain, but the 'madness' everyone's talking about; nah, maybe not so."

By now there was a large bouquet of mini recorders spread out before Martin, capturing his words. Martin spotted them and steered his words more directly towards them, like a bee homing in on a flower.

"The Pit has a reputation that it's useless at keeping a diary," he continued. "It's certainly no Bridget Jones, that's for sure. People and events come and go, and there's no records; not that I can find anyway. It's all been clandestine, hidden. Like some drug trade on the street. A life exchanged for thirty quid with a rapid sleight of hand. The shadowy figure disappears, and nobody remembers, and nobody really wants to. There's no tallies, accounts; data. So that's the first point about what I'm going to do – this time there will be. Things will be recorded, set down. I'll be teched up to the eyeballs. There'll be a 'control centre' in the club, somewhere to collect all the data. And yes, I've read the petition; examined the particulars of the make-life-incredibly-dull campaign. I've seen the local councillors and politicians scurrying around to protect themselves. Restrictions are obviously on their way. So if you're asking, 'Why now? What's the rush?' Well, there's your answer. I'm not sitting around waiting for all that to arrive."

Martin paused here. An expression of excitement transformed his face. He smiled slightly and scanned the lines of faces gazing up at him.

"So, what's it *really* like down there?" he mused. He looked sideways, away from the group as images seemed to fill his head. He panned out a scene with two opposing sweeps of his hands.

"There are roads that spiral down," he began again, almost a hint of pride in his voice.

"They're not all little country lanes though. Some of them are the width of dual carriageways, and there are over twenty miles of them in total. Halfway down, cut into the rock, there's a plateau, and on that plateau, there's a whole warehouse the size of a large B&Q. It's got its own marshalling yard and everything – but no trolleys, stressed-out, arguing couples or DIY-ers who don't quite fit."

He faced his audience squarely again, almost like a tour guide who's desperate to impart some facts and knowledge to their charges.

"If there was no water in the Pit, you could land an Airbus A380 in it quite comfortably – and then take off again without applying the brakes. You could do a few circuits, have a look around and then land again. Lower down, there's a string of pylons, some still with their severed cables dangling down. Then there's a ladder, one hundred feet tall, climbing up and going nowhere, its upper part left protruding out into what must have been the open air. No one knows why. There's miles of old tunnels, a strange junk yard of ninety or so abandoned cars, and talk of a skeleton hanging from a tree. And then there's beyond, where everything carries on to; right down to the bottom; that secret, alluring place where nobody's ever been. Best guess is it's one hundred and thirty metres down, but it's probably more; because as no one's been there yet, no one's actually sure."

Martin smiled again, but cheekily this time.

"And so that's where I come in," he went on. "And while we're dispelling rumours, let's deal with another one – the one that says I'll be diving on my own. Well, that one's easily sorted – because I will be, despite all that's happened; that's the truth of it, plain and simple. And why? – Because no one will come with me. But let's be fair; I can't expect everybody to be as crazy as me now, can I?"

Martin lingered a little now. He lowered his line of sight from the group assembled in front of him and fixed it on the floor. It was as if he was ruminating over the next words he was about to utter, checking them; confirming them ahead of their sounding. A few of the journalists shuffled as if anticipating that something awkward was about to follow, like some awful outpouring or breakdown of some kind. Martin looked up again, and their relief was tangible. "I've thought long and hard about if it's worth it," he carried on, the puncture in the tyre repaired, the journey resumed. "About what could happen to me, why I'm doing it; if I really should? So, I've been honest with myself, asked blunt questions and received honest answers. And that decision-making part of me, that committee, auditor, managing director, high court judge still concurs, agrees, gives me permission, says 'go'. And so I am, before the Pit closes, the fences go up, the off-ences are created, and the chance to reach that magical, unconquered place is gone for good."

Martin appeared now like someone who's said all that they had come to say, that their task was now complete, their obligation fulfilled. There was a resolute confidence covering his face like a mask, and his tone suggested that his briefing was ending – and it was.

"Thank you all once again for coming here today," he said kindly, and then exited the room.

Martin had begun to drift as he'd descended further into the darkness of the Pit. Although the flooded quarry was technically a static mass of water, there were still currents which existed, not rapids or tides, but the differences in temperature between the surface and the levels lower down were enough to create a gentle thermal deviation. Martin sensed this alteration to his course and swam a few strokes to his left to return back to his original track.

He stopped again and gathered his bearings, while checking the readouts on his equipment. Positioned upright now, he spoke into the microphone.

"They were certainly right about the cold," he advised, sounding laboured, "it's pretty intense." He looked about him again. "The viz is amazing though." He pivoted his head left. "I can see more of the pylons now. I thought they'd be the smaller ones, but they're not. They're marching way off into the distance like giants." He faced forwards once more. "I'm at one hundred and fifteen metres now and all I can see below me is" – he looked cautiously down past his feet – "nothing."

Martin lifted his gaze from what could quite easily have been infinity beneath him. He took a couple of long, slow, grateful breaths, and a blameless smile of acceptance came to his face.

"I *do* have a problem though," he said remarkably calmly as the glass on his mask began to haze. Anyone looking in would have seen his features begin to blur. It would be like peering in through an unheated shop window on a bleak winter's morning.

"My regulator's freezing up," he informed anyone listening, only now the thinnest slice of concern riding in his voice. "The agents are good and the separator's working properly. Maybe it's the pressure difference or something. I've already tried the spare, but hardly anything's getting through. Reckon I've got about a minute until everything stops altogether."

Martin's face changed now. He was pained, immediately fearful.

"I'm gonna have to make it back up," he declared. Now he was like a man who hears a strange noise. Following his senses, he fully expects there to be a kitten hiding behind the door, but when he finally plucks up the courage to open it, he finds a dragon residing there. "Jesus," he whimpered. "I'm so bloody, bloody cold ..."

And then he was distracted, almost mercifully so; something out to his right seizing his attention, diverting it from the terror that was now building horrendously inside him. He squinted through his mask to get a better view of what it was, fighting through the gloom, and as he focused on it, he seemed instantly more at ease.

"I can see something coming," he announced down his mic. "I'm not sure what it is." And then even calmer now, his voice was softer; content. "It has a strange *draw*, like an *appeal*. I feel like I should greet it, embrace it; welcome it in. It's like I know it, and it knows me." Martin's voice was tranquil now. He sounded secure, comforted and utterly at peace. "I have no fear now of anything at all," he said.

CHAPTER ELEVEN

Martin would remember many things during this time. What he saw next was almost like a dream; that favourite place revisited, a warm seat by the fire, a place in which to seek solace – something to detract from the pain and fear of the journey yet to come.

The house was huge. It was attractive too, imposing, with four large bay windows, two either side of the central front door, arranged on two storeys. It was built in the 1930s and had generous land to the front and rear. Its roof was slated and grand, and had two twisted brick chimney stacks situated at opposing ends. It was finished in an equal mix of exposed brick and pebble-dash, which was painted an interesting off-yellow colour. The front lawn and borders were impeccably well looked after, and the broad, central, gravel drive was completely devoid of weeds.

Martin was younger here. He was twenty-nine, and he looked fresher, but there was a veil of sadness about his countenance as he drove his powerful Subaru briskly down the lanes. He had a map open on the passenger seat, and every so often he'd glance down at it, checking his bearings as the junctions and crossroads whizzed by. A final right turn and he slowed, his eyes tearing at the letters on the nameplates of the houses on this affluent road. Calypso crept past his side window and with a grateful smile, he stopped and reversed back. He waited by the entrance to the drive for a few seconds, as if he was wondering if he was allowed in, but seeing no gates, he obviously concluded that he was.

The angular corners of the smart, greyish-white gravel cracked together as the tyres of his car compacted it. Some of the stones squeaked oddly as the pressure became more intense. All their noises ceased as Martin pulled to a halt.

The graceful, sweeping arches above the windows were mirrored over the front door too. However, this door was more like one you'd find guarding an old, quaint village church than a house. But the door suited the house well, and commanded an instant respectability to the place. It was solid oak and heavy with a fine, bold, brass handle. To its left was a matching doorbell. Martin pushed it, and what sounded like an orchestra broke out and echoed down the vacuous hall inside. After a few seconds, patiently trodden footsteps approached from the other side, and the door was opened by a woman in her mid-fifties.

She had the kind of smile that would have made the Devil turn good again, and she bestowed this willingly on Martin as soon as she saw him. She had a look of the showbiz about her, a hint of a previous glamorous, glitzy life that was far removed from her apparent profession now. She was medium height, rounding more than she would have liked perhaps, but she was still very attractive. Her eyes scanned Martin's features, and her expression changed slightly, as if she'd quickly picked up on his melancholy state of mind, so that she wore an overlay of compassion.

"Martin?" she questioned, benignly.

"Yes, hi," Martin responded. The woman hesitated and then smiled warmly again.

"So, you decided to choose a pedigree then?" she said.

"Yes," Martin answered, "I've had enough mongrels in my life recently, I'm afraid."

The woman placed a pause in their embryonic conversation. She nodded slightly as she studied him and although they were complete strangers, it was as if she understood exactly where he was coming from, as if she immediately identified that there might be a story attached to this visitor in front of her – and there was.

Martin had been in a relationship for the last five years. He'd fallen in love with a beautiful, lively girl called Lizzie. She was intelligent and funny, and Martin had pretty much mapped out his whole life in front of him like some glorious treasure map with her marking the 'X'. She apparently held a copy of it too, but she had a dangerous seam of boredom running through her, like a volatile high explosive. Martin was aware that he had to keep her interest, but this could be incredibly hard work. She was a thirsty engine with a big tank. And of course, the risk Martin ran with this was running out of fuel. At times, he appeared more like her entertainments manager than her partner and lover. And in this world of hidden booty, there were freak storms which could run a ship aground. Then of course there were the pirates, patrolling the waters, scouring the bays and coves, seeking out their next victims.

And how it had devastated Martin when she'd ended it as she had. He'd discovered them by chance together in town one afternoon, hand in hand, shopping together, her laden with Versace and Gucci, and Blackbeard laden with Hugo Boss.

Martin had confronted her politely about it later that evening, after he'd tried to call her for two hours straight, and she'd eventually picked up her phone. Weirdly, within the course of the previous twelve hours, he suddenly felt like some pervert pestering her rather than her potential future husband. A future which had seemed entirely possible just the day before. Was this man an old flame perhaps, one last outing for old-time's sake? Maybe he was an over-affectionate brother she'd inadvertently failed to mention? But no, none of these. In fact, their conversation was rather short and to the point. She told Martin that she'd, 'Got bored of them and so done something about it'. And just before the phone went dead, those last words of hers, 'Oh, and don't bother to call me again, because Paul won't like that very much.'

It was as if Martin had agreed to participate in some game or competition, only he wasn't aware of it. The break-up ripped him apart, and its effects were immediate. Everything suffered; work, other friends, anyone. It made him edgy and unpredictable. Everyone treated him differently now. They kept him at a distance, like a Molotov cocktail with its fuse lit, ready to be thrown. It took him some weeks to bring his alcohol consumption down below seven pints of lager a day. But he did eventually manage it. Slowly, bit by bit, he'd found the strength to fight back, to douse the blaze, to find his old self again. He started to make decisions which benefited him for a change, and being here at the kennels today was the result of one of them.

"Shall we have a look at him then?" the woman asked, as she reached sideways to a coat hook behind the door and pulled off a trendy quilted jacket.

"Yes, that'd be great, thanks," Martin replied, and while putting on her coat, the woman squeezed through the gap Martin had made for her. As she passed him, Martin helped her on with the remainder of the coat, assisting with a particularly difficult sleeve.

"Thanks," she said gratefully, and led them down a small path which followed the side of the house.

The kennels were perhaps not as people might have expected them to be. Many minds would conjure up images of near-prisons, garlanded in squalor. These were very different, however. The whole set-up was more like a Sandals luxury holiday resort; but for dogs. One of the three full-time staff members passed them coming the other way as he was leaving the facility. He looked content and smart, and he smiled at the woman more as if she was his friend than his employer.

"He looks happy," Martin remarked, as the man almost skipped on his way.

"Oh, yes," the woman answered, "everyone wants to work here. I think a lot of it is about how I run the place," she added, and then stopped and turned to face Martin. "It's always the dogs first, and then it's us. That's always the way it's been. It's a love rather than a business really," she said, and then carried on her way again.

Fifty metres later and they'd arrived at the kennels themselves.

"But we don't call them 'kennels', we refer to them as 'accommodation'," the woman clarified, "because that's what they are."

There were twenty 'accommodations' in total, all detached with their own large, fenced, exercise squares, which led back into a nicely designed wooden living space.

"They have plenty of room, as you can see," the woman continued. "Inside there's a place to sleep and, if they need it, there's central heating too. We'll let ourselves in through here," she advised, and she opened a clear plastic-fronted door. Beyond, lay what looked like a sizeable porch of a house.

It felt warm inside as they entered, and she closed the door quickly behind them again to keep in the heat. Past the porch was access to the living space proper. This was situated behind kind-looking, green fencing, which gave the animals sight of the world outside.

"I think he's sleeping," the woman whispered gently, peering carefully in at a small, prostrate figure on the floor some three metres away from them. "The rest of the litter sold very quickly as you know, and so now this little chap is all on his own."

As they approached the animal, the woman smiled affectionately, almost as if the creature was her own child.

"It still amazes me how beautiful they are," she said, and then she looked at Martin with an almost threatening expression. "How anyone can hurt them I'll never know," she said, and she held the look for a while as if she was assessing him one last time. And then she spoke more warmly again, "Shall we go and say hello?"

The German shepherd puppy was eleven weeks old. He had dark and light brown markings which were evenly balanced on his coat, which was thick and well-groomed. As Martin and the woman stopped next to him, he woke and after giving out a cute yawn, he studied them with his deep, soulful, brown eyes. He seemed to recognise the woman, and suddenly his little body sprang to life, and he bounded over to greet her. She squatted down to be closer to him, stroking his head and then kissing him softly. It was as if she realised in that moment she was finally losing him. It was the most extraordinary display of love and sadness at the same time.

"Good boy, Simba," she praised, and then regained her composure and stood again and turned to Martin. "My niece and I were watching an old copy of the *Lion King* together a few weeks ago. After it had finished, she asked me if I could name one of the new doggies 'Simba'. I explained that it was a name better suited to a cat, albeit a big one. 'But it's a lovely name,' she insisted – and so here we are."

"It *is* a lovely name," Martin reassured her gently. "And I think he's even more beautiful than that little cub." Then without showing any fear, Simba ambled confidently over to Martin and began nuzzling his ankles. It was as if they'd known each other for years. The woman looked down at the puppy, now appearing more than a little relieved.

"Usually he's a bit hesitant with strangers, but blatantly not with you," the woman noted kindly. Martin gazed at the puppy and smiled, looking as if he was about to melt suddenly.

"He's such a lovely little fellah," he cooed. The woman laughed happily.

"Come on," she said, bending down and picking the puppy off the floor, "let's get you two properly introduced." She gestured with a nod for Martin to ready his hands, and then she placed Simba in the cup he'd formed. Martin's eyes filled with tears as the tiny animal licked his face. The woman clearly noticed.

"It looks like it's not so much a case of you choosing him, but of him choosing you," she observed warmly, and gave Simba a final, enduring kiss.

And so this is how they were for the remainder of their lives together. Martin and Simba were inseparable, two futures colliding, changing each other; intertwining willingly and permanently on the lifting of a latch on the gate of a kennel in a leafy, well-heeled, Surrey suburb on an inconspicuous Saturday afternoon.

Their lives set off on its course; first as a puppy in the back garden, lively as wildfire, happy as a birthday party. Them playing with a football together, Simba's teeth eventually bursting through the thin plastic as his jaws grew stronger and stronger. Then, their evenings in the bar of the local pub; Martin supping on his pint with Simba curled up by his feet, hijacking the hearts of the passing traffic in lorry-loads. And now, no longer a puppy, Simba as the strong, dominant male, controlling the acres of the park where he ran, eagerly protecting his owner from anyone who roamed too close. And then later, finally in his autumn years, when the longer walks became too much, Martin slowing the pace as age and the waning endurance in Simba's legs began to show: And then finally that dreadful closing of the day.

Simba remained in Martin's life long after he passed away. They had ten wonderful years together. They were the same soul, the same entity. Nothing or no one had ever come or would ever be that close in Martin's life again.

CHAPTER TWELVE

The country lanes were cruel on Fiona's car as she raced through them. She clipped kerbs and collided with protruding branches from the neighbouring hedges as she careered on her way. She almost lost control on one particular bend as it appeared unexpectedly out of the gloom, then tightened impossibly in on itself like a wound-up clock spring. The type of car she was driving didn't help either. It was a basic Ford, high miles-per-gallon, four-door family saloon, which had all the road-holding of a Victorian pram. There was no upgraded suspension or brakes to make her journey more pleasurable and safer, so she'd just have to wrangle on as best she could.

She'd had to break away from work. She'd feigned a bizarre, temporary illness and now she was driving like a mad woman, battling against time. Unsurprisingly, this wasn't the way she normally drove, but there was something in Martin's question to her about 'Monday' from those days before that was still troubling her. She couldn't put it to one side, put it down or extinguish it. And it was now *that* Monday, 10.30 in the morning to be exact, and what had started as a nibble on her brain had turned into a ravenous feast now the day had actually arrived.

She'd tried Martin's mobile a few times, but it had simply rung out to his answering machine. She'd also contacted a couple of dive club members, but neither knew of Martin's whereabouts either. She'd tried Martin's work too, and they'd told her he was on leave. It was when she'd phoned the two dive club members back and discussed her concerns that they'd all agreed to get to the quarry as fast as they could.

John was the first to arrive. He was a large, rather jolly looking man in his mid-forties. He stood bear-like and had immense strength and impossibly broad shoulders. He was one of the more experienced divers in the club. He'd entered the clubhouse to find Martin's equipment all set up and streaming out data. He'd also found the small loudspeaker on the desk next to the screen, but when he'd placed his ear near it, all he could hear was the faint hiss of static.

Phil, the other diver, arrived two minutes later and then Fiona, her car ominously smelling of burning oil. Once all together, they gathered around the laptop and scrutinised it hurriedly – and then all came to the same conclusion.

In one rapid burst, they fled to the small beach outside, scanning the surface of the water furiously. And then they saw something floating one hundred metres or so out from the shore. It looked like an old log that had been swept down by the winter floodwaters from the moors above. It was motionless and appeared dead. At its crown was a bright yellow, inflated diver's survival vest.

John sprinted over to the tied-up inflatable boat which was secured to the small jetty they'd built. On his way over, he fumbled for and then found the keys to the padlocks which unlocked the thick, uncompromising chain, which wrapped itself around the engine and then a large metal stave like a boa constrictor.

Soon the Evinrude 40 was running and ready, and the three of them leapt into the craft and raced out to the floating bundle they'd spotted. A perilous ten minutes had already expired since Martin's voice had last sounded down the small but feisty loudspeaker back in the clubhouse.

"Call an ambulance!" Fiona screamed to John as soon as they laid Martin on the bank and she looked into his lifeless, greying face. "Call a bloody ambulance!" Then she bent down closer. "Can you hear me, Martin?" she yelled, "Can you hear me?"

They'd fought to find comfort for Martin, where to place him among all that, brutal, hard rock. They'd decided they needed to get him set down as soon as they could, and so a sparsely grassed patch of earth close by the water's edge would have to serve as a bed.

It had started to rain, and the large, full drops bounced off Martin's skin as if he was now just some material object, like stone or wood. There was no reaction from him at all to the discomfort they should have been inflicting on him. But that would be a result of the state of unconsciousness that had settled on him now, willingly seizing his body with death waiting in the wings, wanting to take it for its own. It was as if this siege had already begun because the base of his nostrils was starting to turn blue.

"Martin!" Fiona called again, taking his head in her hands as if he was somehow faking his condition. With still no response, she felt for a pulse on the vein on his neck. But there was nothing there.

"Fuck!"

She placed her hand in front of Martin's mouth to check for breath, but again there was an absence of anything.

"Jesus."

Quickly, she lowered her head, turning it to one side so her ear was directly against his mouth, but all she heard was silence.

"Martin!"

Moving down his body, she placed her ear flat against his chest, checking for a heartbeat – which wasn't there. She was trembling now as panic was clearly setting in.

"No!" she wailed dismally. She looked about her now, desperately thinking about what to do next. Questioning her last findings, she put her head back on Martin's chest, this time wrenching her long, straying hair clear in case it might be interfering with their contact in some way.

"Shit. Fucking shit!" she cried, but still that dreadful void.

Now frenzy took her over. Her eyes darted wildly about as if she was trying to remember something; some past course in a distant time, some details lodged in her head, some small point; any small point, the basics of CPR perhaps.

"What do I do?" she squealed. "What do I do!"

Then suddenly something seemed to enter her head. She moved back and kneeled over Martin, placing her hands, one over the other in the centre of his chest, and she began compressions. She counted aloud as she did so, two strong lunges down per second. After fifteen of these, she stopped and listened for breathing once more. She was pleading with him now.

"Martin!"

Moving away from his chest, she pinched his nose, and after covering his mouth with hers, she blew a long, deep breath into him.

"Come on!" she shrieked as she watched his chest rise, fall, but then stay down. She delivered twenty more frantic strokes.

"Bloody hell, Martin; come on!" she screeched. Then her ear on his chest for another time, feverishly listening for that sound, but again nothing but silence, save the trickle of the rain against his face.

"Shit," she said softly, as the severity of the situation crashed fully into her. Now any composure she'd managed to muster had disappeared.

"He's gone, he's gone!" she bawled hysterically. She put her hands to her head as she looked hopelessly around her.

"Fuck. He's gone!" she sobbed.

CHAPTER THIRTEEN

There was a mixture of fascination, envy, and for some, disdain. The motorcycle stood with the others in the large car park that surrounded the café, but the small crowd had noticeably gathered around this particular machine.

Martin watched them through the window while sipping his tea. The group consisted of both men and women, all aged over thirty, and they viewed the bike from several angles. Some circled it. It was if they were inspecting an animal of some kind, a prize bull perhaps, like a farmer might do before the start of a cattle auction.

They examined the components of the model in turn; the engine, tyres, dials and the huge tank of the Suzuki GSX1300R Hayabusa, some of them nodding in appreciation occasionally. An owner of a huge, shiny-piped Harley came over momentarily and muttered something to himself, his devil-dark leathers building his frame, making a bona fide Hells Angel out of a chartered accountant for the day. The remainder of the group turned around to face him; one of them spoke just two words, and the Harley rider suddenly wandered off again. But such was the reaction to this bike; it had a tendency to polarise.

The Ponderosa Café was situated on the top of the Horseshoe Pass above Llangollen in North Wales. It was popular with bikers because of the thrills the road here offered with its sharp bends, interesting straights and steep inclines. In the summer months especially, the area would be festooned with riders, all keen to sample the fantastic views and test their skills. This lure was no less diminished for Martin, and so he'd brought his 'Busa' on this mission today.

He'd started out earlier in the day, twenty miles away, up near Chester. There was a main two-lane arterial road that scorched its way south, linking the main towns along its routes. The bike had left everything behind as he'd accelerated away from the traffic lights, collecting some serious G-force as he did so. There was very little that could match this monster's performance, making it one of the fastest motorcycles ever made.

It wasn't long before Martin met the smaller A-roads, which wound their way through to Llangollen. This was a pretty market town which had the privilege of having the captivating and sometimes dangerous River Dee running through its centre. To its side was a steam train with several miles of dedicated track, which followed the contours of the extending valleys up into the hills. In winter this would turn into the 'Santa Express', and it would be crammed with hundreds of excited children, all rattling and chuffing their way up to a Winter Wonderland, which had been constructed seven miles away at the next station. Along the route, the great man himself would move through the carriages with his entourage of elves, smiling. He'd endlessly ask the same question about who'd been good and who'd been bad during the last year, and give out presents to all the kids, irrespective of their individual answers.

Martin finished his tea, left his mug on the counter, and nodded to the man standing behind it. "Thanks. See you again," he said cheerily. The man waved and then Martin went back outside, carrying his crash helmet in his hand.

He wandered back to the bike as he zipped up his bespoke racing leathers with their vibrant colours, the decals of the Busa, and the protective carbon fibre sections over his elbow, spine and knees. He said hello to the group who were still clustered around his machine as he took out his keys. They all returned his greeting in various ways, and then one of them approached him somewhat nervously. "Is she nice?" he asked.

Martin paused and smiled. "Lovely," he answered proudly.

"Thought she might be," the man in his forties replied, sounding jealous. "I had a go on one once," he confessed. "Bit too fast for me though, I'm afraid. I'd end up killing myself."

"Know what you mean," Martin quipped. "But you just have to give her the respect she deserves, and you'll be all right," he advised, sounding a little like some old Indian chief giving advice to his young braves – and sounding a tad pretentious too.

The reference to dying on the bike passed over most of the group on that clear and beautiful morning, and to Martin too; but possibly it shouldn't have. His journey had its return leg ahead of it, and it was on this section that the almost throwaway line by another rider would later take on special and serious relevance.

Martin mounted the broad, black, logoed seat of the bike, and connected the straps on his gloves. Keys in, alarm disabled, choke fully on, neutral selected, clutch in, then he depressed the starter button. The motor whizzed happily and fast, and the cylinders of the 1300cc engine lit up, and a massive roar consumed the car park. He waved to the group who were still watching him, then he engaged first gear and sped off heading back down the pass.

He negotiated Llangollen easily enough, weaving his way through the queuing traffic, much to the frustration of the drivers who were trapped there. Soon he was on the main A-road again, and it was here where he nearly died.

It's a common problem with some drivers that they simply don't use their mirrors. It seems as if there's some strange logic being employed – that if they don't see something, then it doesn't exist. There's a defiance of science and logic somehow.

It's akin to someone not looking at something that terrifies them. If they can't see it then surely it's not there?

Further down the road, the bends straightened, and the speed limit increased to 60 mph. The lorry in front of Martin now was a relatively small one, but it would turn out later that this would be an advantage. With nothing coming the other way, Martin deliberately placed himself within view of the lorry's driver. Martin could see the driver in the vehicle's wing mirror, and so the driver could also see him. Martin signalled right and began his manoeuvre to overtake, but halfway past, the lorry suddenly swerved hard right in an attempt to overtake the car in front of him. Martin, in turn, had to swerve hard himself and for a moment he was passing two vehicles lined up side by side. With the road narrowing and a lamp post fast approaching, Martin had no choice but to twist frantically on the throttle and screech by the lorry on its outside. The space to do this was so tight that he had to duck down under the wing mirror of the lorry. His helmet clunked against the underside of it, and it was only now that the driver of the lorry realised he was there.

Behind him, Martin saw the lorry pull in heavily left again, the driver clearly abandoning his former intentions. The lorry then weaved slightly, as if the driver was now suffering from some element of shock. Martin cursed under his breath as he raced clear and away to safety. He laughed slightly at the discomfort of the driver. He wished they could have swapped places and the lorry driver could have shared his experience; seeing that solid pillar of concrete accelerating towards him, threatening to slice him vertically in two. One last look in his mirror and the lorry was gone. The vehicle had pulled into a lay-by, the driver now recovering possibly, taking time to consider what he'd just done.

This recollection seemed to shake Martin from the inside, and it forced his eyes open. He awoke, lying prostrate and weak in the hospital bed. He'd been dreaming, deeply. All sorts of memories had been running through his head. He looked scared for a moment, lost, as if he was trying to identify the situation he now found himself in. Then other more recent events seemed to come back to him, and his expression changed as he worked out exactly where he was.

CHAPTER FOURTEEN

There were no windows in this room. It was almost as if things were meant to be contained in there, like the solitary confinement cell in a prison, or a strongroom, or a store for dangerous chemicals. There was a deliberate intention in the architecture. It was a place where things stayed or ended, and only with another's permission could that be altered.

The bed looked odd, almost because it fitted Martin so precisely. His head was nestled centrally on the snow-white pillow, which was plumped up to perfection. His feet had ample space too before the bottom of the bed framed his toes. He was in balance, made possible by the mechanics of the clever contraption in which he lay, with its self-regulating, intelligent machinery.

His face carried a grim hue, and it was marked in places, especially on his forehead where the top of his mask had been. This was a deep and sorrowful red colour, and imitated the mark of a branding iron. Down his left cheek, there was a curious line of what appeared to be pin-pricks. He'd received these from a stray bramble that had clawed him in his evacuation to the bank. On his chin, there was a rounded, purple bruise, which resembled a beard. It looked painful and would be when he fully awoke.

This process had already begun and ironically, Martin would be listening to the very same sounds Rob was presented with in those final, depressing moments of his life. In an odd way, his and Martin's lives now became weirdly identical because of these shared events. There'd be no missing these sounds now for Martin because he was late. On this occasion, he'd be hearing them from the alarming position of a victim, and not a potential observer.

Fiona glanced over from her seat, which was next to Martin's bed. She looked like someone who's endured an ordeal, some disaster or other, and who's emerged on the other side of it – but only just.

"Well, at least you're not blue anymore," she commented wryly, managing a slight smile; seeming pleased that Martin was finally escaping unconsciousness. Martin fixed his eyes on her and waited for them to focus, as if they were part of a camera lens that was fighting for a smarter image before the shutter closes.

"How come I'm not?" he asked, trying for a grin but obviously failing, "or worse – a rather unattractive shade of grey?"

"Someone finally found the defibrillator," Fiona advised him. Martin felt his chest just after as she passed this information on to him. "We got it on you as quick as we could and then you eventually started breathing again, you awkward little bastard. Then we swapped a mossy bank for a hospital." She shook her head. "You seemed hell bent on ending up in ICU and so, well," – she looked around the room, taking her time – "here you are."

Martin didn't respond, rather he looked away from her and down into the inert covers of his bed. He seemed momentarily impressed by the crisp, well-washed material. Fiona leaned back in her chair, a question taking over her expression now and, judging by how serious she looked, it had been lingering in her head for some considerable time.

"So," she began carefully, "what did you 'see', exactly?"

Martin's diversion clearly helped him, and he seemed more
at ease as he grew more accustomed to his surroundings. He
looked relieved too, like someone in the Blitz, looking
skywards; listening, convinced that the bombardment is finally
over.

He maintained his gaze on the linen for another fifteen
seconds before he answered her. But even then, it was as if he
was being deliberately vague, hiding something that only he
knew about; like a prospector with a newly discovered, fabulous
find.

"I don't know," he drawled somewhat lazily, "It was
strange." He shrugged his shoulders. "Maybe it was just oxygen
starvation or something."

Fiona studied him for a while. She looked both annoyed and
intrigued at the same time.

"Possibly," she replied, sounding a little deflated by his
response. "It can do weird, crazy things."

Martin's face softened. He had a kinder mien now. He'd
been changed. The way a simple, plain square box is changed
into a present by colourful wrapping paper and a beautifully
tied bow.

"It *was* stunning though," he uttered dreamily. "I floated five
feet above the roads that go winding down. It was like I was in
a … hovering car or something. It was surreal. I could almost
picture everyone still working down there. It was as if I
suddenly became part of it."

Fiona pulled one of her famous levelling faces, as she
ordered in another squadron of bombers.

"You damn nearly did," she reminded him. "So what
happened with the regulator? Did you suddenly turn into an
imbecile or something?"

Martin smiled as he looked at her.

"I've always been one of those, haven't I?"

"More of one then?"

"The cold's a real bitch." Martin continued, more solemnly now. He sounded like a veteran recalling some campaign they'd been on. "I've never felt anything like it before. It almost needs proper Arctic kit down there. After a while, I had no choice. I just had to torpedo to the surface – and I'm afraid my system didn't like that very much."

"We know." Fiona resembled a school teacher now when the whole class are late with their homework again. "You almost died."

Martin rolled his eyes.

"Here we go," he mumbled.

"But it's true."

"I'm not a five-year-old, Fiona."

"You're right; you're not – because a five-year-old would have considerably more common sense than you." She leaned in closer to him. "Don't you *ever* dive alone down there again, Martin!" she scolded.

Martin's reply was odd.

"Right," he said after a pause and a telling smile.

Fiona was puzzled.

"What?" she asked, a certain amount of trepidation in her voice now. Martin's smile broadened.

Fiona's puzzlement deepened.

"Well, being *so* much of an imbecile, what would you *expect* me to do?" he asked hazily, and then added reasoning to his next words: "Look, after what's just happened to me the suits'll be clamouring over themselves to close the place down now, won't they? And besides, I'd only be doing what you were telling me to do."

"I'm not 'telling' you to do anything."

"Yes you are. You just told me again. 'Don't dive alone', you said," Martin quoted, and then took a completely obscure turn on the route of their somewhat baffling conversation. "Forks," he declared.

"Sorry?" Fiona was really struggling to keep up now. Martin grinned before carrying on.

"I was always told to place my peas on top of my fork, not to scoop them up in 'an uncouth manner'. Of course, that's bollocks. If you're shovelling shit – should you be unfortunate enough to have to – you wouldn't use the top of the shovel, you'd use its other side, its depression into which things are designed to fall. Unless you deliberately want shit in your boots, that is."

"And your point is …?"

"That what people tell you isn't always correct."

"What the hell are you babbling on about, Martin!"

Martin sat as upright in the bed, getting as close to Fiona as he could manage.

"Come on, buddy with me, Fiona," he almost pleaded. "I've asked you before, but now it's different."

"How?" There was an element of anger building in Fiona's voice.

"Because we're running out of time."

"And my answer's still the same – you've got to be bloody joking!"

"What have you got to lose?"

Fiona looked around the room in disbelief and then she returned to Martin.

"My life!" she shouted out incredulously.

"Maybe," Martin answered her equitably, "But if you did do it, you might lose something else more important than that, to you at the moment anyway."

"And what could be more important than my life?"

"Come on, you know."

Fiona laughed slightly.

"Do I?"

"Yes, you do." Martin fixed her with a stare. "Your fear," he said curtly.

Fiona looked suddenly discovered. She was silenced instantly, and she leant back on her seat again, like someone retreating, finding space and safety.

"It's taken me a little time to discover it," Martin went on, speaking more softly now, "but I know it's there."

Fiona wriggled now. Her face was sheened with a blameless expression.

"What fear?" she asked dismissively.

Martin didn't reply, rather he simply stared at her and held her in his imprisoning gaze, which emanated pity, understanding and the truth.

CHAPTER FIFTEEN

It wasn't so much a scream as a long, extended wail. It came from the corridor outside, and it consumed the whole building, and to a large degree, all the people inside it too. The doctor in front of Fiona was included in that group. He looked up at the ceiling suddenly as the sound barged into the room. He concentrated on it, fixing its source possibly, and then he relaxed again as he seemed to identify its owner. He looked back at Fiona, not apologising for breaking the flow in her conversation so brutally.

"My 'symptoms'?" Fiona carried on, obviously frustrated now. "They're the same as before – but worse." She eyed him coldly. "Or don't you remember what they were?"

The doctor paused and stared back at her for a while. He didn't answer her immediately but made it clear from the look on his face that he would respond at his own pace, in his own time, and that there was no way she would intimidate him.

"So," he finally answered, his words accompanied by a slight, sly smile, "why don't you tell me again?"

The smile soon withered, however, and he looked over to his notes rippling down the screen of the computer monitor in front of him. He gave the impression that he was peeved, already bored by their interaction as if he had these all day and Fiona's was the next in a very long line of similar rants, complaints and worthless whining. Fiona willingly returned his veiled hostility. She couldn't match his truly weary appearance though; not unless she'd worked fourteen hours a day for the last week with the promise of more with the rumour of a flu epidemic on its way. On the basis of this rumour, it seemed like everyone had flocked to the surgery convinced they now had the plague. And this was a sustained existence for the relatively young doctor who was listening to her now. But again, Fiona could never have picked this up, or known that the doctor's two young children were beginning not to recognise him as easily as they once did.

Fiona took a moment to prepare herself; what she was about to recount to him would be painful for her.

"I feel totally detached from reality," she began. "I get breathless. I have heart palpitations, and I feel dizzy." Fiona stopped here. She took a break like a climber does as they ascend a steep hill, picking their way through the sharp, loose rocks and the brambles, the extra dexterity demanded by them simply adding to the exhaustion. After a few moments, she carried on. "I feel like fainting, and I sweat like crazy. I feel completely out of control. It's like I'm having a full-blown panic attack or something."

Because she'd started to speak, to impart her experience to the doctor, it seemed easier for her to lose some of her former aggression and as a result, she opened up a little more – possibly with the misguided expectation that the doctor somehow now actually gave a shit.

"I feel lost," she carried on. "It's like I don't know what to do. I embarrass myself in front of other people by the way I behave. I find myself crying, shaking or trembling. I have these terrible thoughts of … death and dying." She was close to tears. "I just feel like running away."

Fiona left a space as she thought about what she'd just said, and it was as if she'd suddenly come to and realised where she was. And as she gathered her senses, she looked almost ashamed of having dropped her barrier, and entered into this confession so readily. But it wasn't long before she returned to being antagonistic once more. Perhaps it was something to do with what she found when she looked at the doctor again; that barren, expressionless, arid desert of a face where only snakes and silly little skipping lizards lived.

"I'm at my wits' end," she continued, deliberately capturing his attention with her steely eyes so he couldn't escape, "and this is my third appointment with you – but nothing ever improves. I've had extremely bad episodes all week leading up to this … 'slot' here today; which I only managed to get after fighting with your bitch of a receptionist for half an hour. I could tell that she just didn't believe me."

The doctor severed the look between them now, her rudeness clearly annoying him. He was making it obvious that a limit had been reached, a border crossed. It's like the moment the bus driver stops his vehicle, applies the air brake, leaves his seat and throws the rolling, abusive drunk off into the gutter. Everybody's suffered this vile individual's antics for the last five appalling miles, but finally it's time to stop – literally. It's only been the driver's compassion and patience that's kept him on for this long. But that's now dissipated and despite the drunk's swearing, threats and protestations, he now has to scramble his way home through the ice and snow. The bus carries on, and everyone is happy again.

"Look," Fiona resumed, calmer now, clearly picking up the doctor's intentions. "The counselling only works so far, the meditation too. It's time to try something stronger." She was emotional again now. "You've got to give me something to end this torture that I'm in. Because it's not just the symptoms of the fear, the anxiety, everything; but how I … function as well. I'm not eating properly now. It's all just junk food. My appetite's barely there. I don't use the gym any more. I don't feel like going out – and never mind about sex. So, I stay in like a bloody hermit. But then it's just me and the curtains, isn't it?

And as nice as they are, I have nowhere to go, nothing to distract me and so the cycle simply runs over on itself again, and the whole thing continues, growing bigger and bigger, wanting and taking more and more of me. I'm really worried about how much is actually left."

Fiona forced a smile, but she was becoming exasperated again, the momentum of her tirade driving her blindly on.

"And you ask me if I'm going through the change?" She sneered, seemingly not caring any more. "No, I'm *not* going through the change. Christ, is that really the best you can do? Well, I suppose it is, isn't it? Or the best you want to do. Too many of us, are there? Sort the 'proper' ones out first? Go on, do it again; turn up this bloody arrogance you have, pat me on my head, smile and send me on my way again. Why not, eh?"

She lowered her head as if her last few sentences had just been played back to her, as if she'd just caught the tail of a very long, extended echo as it bounced around the walls and returned to them both. Consequently, there was regret in her voice now.

"Look, I really *am* at the end of my tether," she reasoned without looking up. "Please, can you just give me something to make things easier?"

There was silence as the doctor didn't reply. After ten more difficult seconds, Fiona lifted her head to find out why. The doctor was looking at his screen once more, tapping out notes on his keyboard, completely ignoring her.

"Right, so that's it, is it?" Fiona blasted out hatefully, looking as if she really wanted to hurt him now. "So there's *nothing* at all that you're willing to give me?"

CHAPTER SIXTEEN

The haze cleared from Fiona's eyes and she returned to the ICU in the hospital once more. Martin saw her climb out from her recollection as if she was a survivor of a car wreck, and he greeted her kindly with a warm, comforting smile.

"I *can* see how strong the fear is in you," he said. Fiona didn't answer. She was plainly still suffering from the shock of her 'accident'. Martin picked this up and, sensibly, he was silent for a while. After a minute, he'd obviously decided it was time to move things on and so he spoke again.

"I was round at my friend's house recently ..."

Fiona cut into him suddenly with a glare. Her eyes read: *"Not another one of your stories!"*

"There *is* a point, trust me," Martin persevered. Fiona turned away and let him carry on "... When his eight-year-old son came into the room. He looked upset, and so his dad broke away from our conversation and talked to him. 'I don't want you to die,' his son said to his dad. 'It'll make me really sad.'

"'Don't be silly. I'm not going to die. Well, not for ages yet,' his dad reassured him.

"'When you're a ghost,' his son went on, 'will you make a special knock, so I know it's you and I won't be frightened?'

"His dad pulled him in close and gave him a big, long, tight, loving hug. He wiped his son's tears away. 'Of course, I will, love. Of course, I will,' he said.

"'Can we practice one now, so I'll know what it'll be?'

"His dad nodded and smiled and created a special knock right there and then and tapped it out on the arm of his chair." Martin extended his right arm and copied the same rhythmic knock on the top of the table next to him.

"'How's that?' his dad asked affectionately.

"His little boy smiled. 'That's great, that's brilliant,' he said, smiling now. 'It makes me feel *so* much better.'"

Martin looked skywards and was briefly lost in thought.

"That wonderful agreement they made," he contemplated, sounding a little soppy. "That transit between worlds. One knock on two doors at the same time; that accord, that permanent bond. Jesus; how I envied that."

When Martin brought his gaze back down to earth, Fiona was facing him.

"So, what has all that got to do with me then?" she challenged him coldly.

Martin looked back at her and replicated her expression.

"If you were as clever as you think you are, you'd already know the answer to your own question," he suggested, with all the subtlety of a ten-pound lump hammer. And then he was softer. "They confronted it, didn't they, Fiona; both of them," he went on, "unlike you. What that little lad did so fantastically was to summarise that fearful unknown. And he created a way for both of them to see into it. Because his fear was one that must be shared by virtually everyone at some point in their lives; that place beyond; the view that can never be seen – until you're actually in the landscape, that is. But he gave himself, and his dad, so much comfort by that device he invented. And we're lucky."

"Really?" Fiona interrupted cynically, with an element of self-pity.

"Yes, because some people have to deliberately ignore or fight off the future, don't they? People with terminal diseases, dreading that day that's coming too soon, the party that's ending prematurely, the cancelled match. There's no point in being frightened of it for them as it will only win if they are. It's like another symptom for them. They have absolutely no option but to confront it."

Martin shuffled in his bed to face forwards again. His countenance changed as he pictured something fondly, and with considerable admiration. Fiona lowered her head and sighed as if she sensed something was coming. She swivelled away from him, settling in, some previous experience perhaps telling her she'd have to accept this, tolerate it for another time; hear him out.

"I see this man in my gym," Martin relentlessly persisted. "He's on crutches, beasting it out, finding ways to use the kit five days a week, despite how whatever has affected him has messed him up. Even his voice has been altered by it; he can only just speak. And then that triumphant day when I heard those words screeching through the air towards me: 'I've done it! I've fucking done it!'

"I turned around to see him standing in the middle of the room, legs bowed, trembling slightly, but no crutches; his arms free in the air for the first time in years possibly. Nothing in his grasp but opportunity; and that wonderful, grateful smile on his face as he took another step, and then one more, like a child walking for the very first time. He made it to the bench-press machine on his own, and then we all cheered, clapped, whooped, punched the air with him. We all felt truly humbled."

Martin found Fiona's eyes again; fixed her.

"And so what of him?" he asked. "What of that man staring right into the face of that malcontent with its too-early, merciless plans there waiting for him?" Martin smiled. "It *can* be done, Fiona," he urged, gently, "faced, adjusted to, put in its place, beaten maybe, I don't know – but you can do it too."

He nodded slowly as he paused.

"We're all going to stare into that face, meet that person," he went on, "but on the *other* side of the door. I'm not going to let that dread … *contaminate* my life now. I'm going to do things while I still can. I'm not knocking quite just yet. Life's path keeps on going right to the edge of the cliff. If we follow that path, then we should follow it to its end – or why did we follow it in the first place?"

Rather than nodding her head, Fiona now shook hers.

"Why do you think everything is always so bloody simple, Martin?" she demanded angrily.

"I don't," Martin retorted, "because there's usually a reason why things happen, isn't there? Things *can* be simple. Look for that first." He gave her a sterner look. "You were very keen to tell me about your grandmother earlier. What was it? Did something happen to her?"

Fiona hesitated as if she was struggling over whether to answer him, if she should answer him; if he had the right to receive an answer from her at all. She decided that he should.

"She died," she half-mumbled.

"When?"

"Recently."

"How recently?"

Martin could see that this event still pained Fiona and that she had difficulty in affording it some reality.

"Six months ago next week," she uttered, battling on.

"You know the date so exactly. Do you feel lost without her, abandoned?"

"No."

"Betrayed perhaps?"

Fiona span around viciously.

"No, never that," she snapped protectively, "not with her."

Martin thought for a moment.

"I'm curious," he probed considerately. "Was she your secret knock?"

Fiona stood and moved away. She faced the far, blank, white wall. Its nothingness appeared to soothe her, and after a while, she spoke again.

"Now everything's in the fast lane on the M1 Motorway on a dark, snowy, awful night," she ruminated sounding hurt. "I'm doing ninety miles an hour; I can't see where I'm going, and I'm just … stuck there hoping for the best." Fiona looked instantly sad. "I suppose I didn't expect it after she'd gone. But then it came, and I realised; the guiding hand, the wisdom; that rock, all gone and, in its place, an ever-increasing panic as hot as molten lead sticking to my roasting, blistering skin." She focused on the skirting board now with its chipped paint from where a stray trolley had rolled into it; an unexpected scar hidden among all that pristine excellence.

"You know," she went on, "having never felt this kind of thing before, I've got absolutely no idea of how to deal with it now. It's almost as if it knows that and so it grows stronger every day, feeding off me like some horrible … *parasite*, still getting stronger – and all because of me."

"So, if we're talking cars," Martin suggested, "I'd say the headlights have gone out. Everything ahead now is a possible threat, a danger; something to be terrified of."

Martin waited before carrying on. He adopted a softer tone now; the kind that's deliberately pitched so as not to offend; because there is a real chance that it might do.

"There's actually a name for the fear you have, Fiona," he began again. "I did some research on it."

"Did you?"

"Yes, it's called chronophobia – the fear of the future. So, what better way of breaking that fear of the unknown by actually going there? Find the switch; put those lights back on again."

Picking up his reference to diving again, Fiona twisted quickly back around to face Martin once more.

"Right," she targeted him harshly. "So, we throw in some more … *hazards* just to make it more comfortable, do we? Lightning, sheet ice, some loose load from a lorry; huge concrete pipes buckaroo-ing down the road towards me? We all just become *totally* irresponsible like you, is that it? Despite all the training, all that knowledge you claim to have understood, even the qualifications you've got; we just ignore it all. Is that what you're saying?"

"No, we use it."

"Really? Is that what we should do? This is all some kind of odd 'utilisation', some 'recycling' project, is it? This obsession with diving on your own – because that's what it will be, because no one else will go with you, including me – which particular textbook did you learn that from because it's in no book I've ever read."

"There comes a time to make a judgement call."

"And that judgement call includes ignoring what everyone is telling you?"

"If I think they're wrong, yes."

"They're not wrong, Martin. They're just looking out for you."

"They're just playing safe, Fiona. That pit has claimed all those lives. All those people trying to discover its secret."

"And that's my point."

"We owe it to them to try!"

"No, we owe it to them to be safe!"

"Is that what they'd want?"

"Having died trying, I reckon, yes."

"And how the hell do you know that?"

"So, you'll risk your life on a question that can't be answered?"

"Well, given what else I'm doing in my life, I might as well do, yes."

"My response is still 'no'. You're on your own."

"And my response is still the same too. I'm not asking for yours or anyone else's permission to try. As soon as I'm right, I'm going to try again. Nobody truly owns that water – and nobody owns me."

Fiona grinned sarcastically.

"Well, bully for you!"

Martin took a moment. He was the calmer of the two of them now.

"And that's *my* point," he replied evenly. Bully for me – bully for you, more like. You're being 'bullied' but you either can't or won't see that. Control that fear you have or it will control you for the rest of your life. And one day you're going to wake up and find that you haven't actually got very much of that life left to be worried about." Martin managed a smile for her despite the bitterness they'd just exchanged. "The buses are leaving the depot, Fiona," he went on gently. "Nothing you can do will stop them. Maybe you should board one of them, take a risk, take a ride – see where they go."

CHAPTER SEVENTEEN

Christmas was almost there, and so the tiresome, annual family meet-up had arrived for another year. These were normally fairly ordinary affairs, and Fiona was nine years old when this episode took place.

Her mother, Deborah, was getting ready for the trek. Of course, she refused to be called 'Debbie' or 'Debs'; that would never do. She insisted on being addressed in the 'full term' as she put it. There was a kind of threat in her voice when she transformed into this heartless pedant. This happened quite frequently and so this odd, authoritarian grimness permeated over almost everything she did, and sadly this trip would be no different; it would have any enjoyment deliberately squeezed out of it like a once succulent orange. All that would be left would be chewy pith, the brutalised remnants of the fruit and bitter, acidic peel. And like with so many of her unfortunate, miserable endeavours, there'd be consequences to deal with afterwards too.

Deborah and her siblings, Abigail and Jonathan, would assemble at one of their houses for some Christmas cheer in the last week before the big day. It was a tradition they'd started a year after they'd all left home. Its intentions had been well-meant initially, but because Deborah was involved, it had naturally evolved into another of her senseless competitions. They were like the nations who host the Olympic Games. Each year the opening and closing ceremonies get increasingly flamboyant and expensive as countries attempt to outdo each other. The true spirit of the games gets drowned in a needless, vast, man-made sea of egos that they deliberately manufacture.

This year's soiree was being held at Abigail's place over in Sheffield. It'd be like the next in the series of a cricket competition. She'd be attempting to bat Deborah's adequate show, from twelve months previously past the boundary and out of the ground. This was already apparent in the invitations she'd had especially hand-crafted and delivered. They were more like works of art than a communication device. She'd commissioned both an artist and calligrapher to design and create the cards; then the private courier would make certain they'd be delivered in exceptionally good time.

Deborah's mother and Fiona's grandmother, Eve, strongly discouraged this behaviour between her children. She'd state this too, kindly of course, but she'd got to that time in her life where her kids naturally knew better than her. They'd hear but not listen, and see but not notice, and Deborah especially shone out as the rudest and coldest of them all.

Things were in a rush as usual, and Fiona, her younger brother, George, and Eve had already been subjected to one of Deborah's standard disproportionate and vile rages. She wasn't very good at coping and yet, even though she seemed to know this, she'd take on things which demanded calmness and coolness in exorbitant measures. Small things would quickly escalate and then would conjoin to form one massive, God-awful situation which was a million, trillion miles away from being anything enjoyable. It was a pity, because these situations could so easily have been fun. It was as if Deborah didn't care about what the results of her actions might be, and so actually this made her incredibly selfish. Those closest to her usually bore the brunt of her appalling and largely inexcusable behaviour. This was why Eve accompanied her whenever she could, and today she was riding shotgun for her grandchildren, protecting them from the worst of it if she could. She was like the bouncer on the door of a nightclub on a lively Saturday night, just waiting to step in.

Given that it was this close to the end of year, the weather was understandably not at its best; all the more reason not to take on the Pennine Hills perhaps. But Deborah had decided that all would be well and so now the four of them and her 'supplies' were wedged into her basic Nissan Micra. Deborah was driving, and the satnav was doing its best to keep her on track. She'd missed a couple of turnings, and so even now they were behind in their schedule. Things were already starting to turn sour as she swore at the device for its error, accusing it of being 'stupid'.

To compensate for the loss of time, they were now thundering down the fast lane of the M56 motorway having headed out of Chester by way of a circuitous and unnecessary route. The salt gritting lorries had already been out by now, which was unusual for this time of day. They normally applied a covering to the roads only once in every twenty-four hours, but given the warnings of the advancing front heading in east from Russia, they were taking extra precautions. Eve had broached the sensitive but obvious subject of the conditions with Deborah back at her house some time before they'd set off, and she raised it again now.

"Do you really think it's worth the risk of travelling all this way, Deborah?" she enquired again, somewhat rebelliously.

Her daughter didn't look at her to respond; she simply glanced in her mirror to check for approaching police cars, as they were now doing ninety-five.

"We're going, and that's final," she answered, as frostily as some of the decaying snowmen they'd passed in the gardens earlier. There'd been a heavy fall in the week previously much to the satisfaction of their builders. "Don't do your usual trick and try and back out at the last moment," Deborah continued in her familiar accusing and insulting tone.

"It's nothing to do with 'tricks'", Eve retorted. "It's more to do with the fact that it might snow again, and you've decided to go over the Snake Pass."

"We'll be fine, I've told you. Just chill, will you?" Deborah said. It was George who had the foolishness to try and break the fiendishly uncomfortable silence that naturally followed.

"Why couldn't Dad come?" he chirped innocently. Deborah's face tightened.

"Because he works in *retail*," she scoffed disparagingly, the corners of her mouth curling up like the edges of old, sliced bread. Eve turned round to face her grandson, smiling as she did so.

"Your daddy manages a big department store in town, love," she reminded him kindly. "This is one of their busiest times of year. He can't just take a day off when he likes," she went on, making it evident that she was fairly and justifiably filling in the gaps left by Deborah's intentionally one-sided reply. Deborah grimaced as she continued to stare ahead through the ever-dirtying windscreen.

"Right," she sneered disbelievingly, implying some conspiracy or other.

Eve fixed her daughter with a rebuking stare. "And *he* didn't want us to come either," she reiterated starkly.

Abigail's house in Sheffield lay just over eighty miles away. She was a lecturer in Economics at the local university, and her husband was a bigwig in construction. Consequently, they competed in the property stakes at a highly respectable level. As a result, their house had a name rather than a number and was situated in one of the grander quarters of the city. The houses here were big and detached with plenty of space between them. They resembled a nice part of London rather than an area of a leading industrial capital. It was here where all the professionals, and some villains, lived in their beautiful, natural, stone-built piles with massive, well-cared-for gardens.

Abigail and her husband's house had three levels with six bedrooms in all. They'd spent a fortune renovating and refurbishing the property over several years. They'd taken a lot of the work on themselves, including most of the grunt work; barrowing earth and waste and filling skips. Deborah always commented that Abigail was snobby and socially obsessed, or 'up her own arse' as she so eloquently put it. But judging by the amount of time, effort and dedication they'd committed to their project, perhaps to a point, she had the right to be.

Back in the car, Deborah and her hostages were heading past Stockport. Here the motorway would weave its way through several interchanges and then the road would narrow to an A-road and begin to negotiate the climb up to the dreaded Snake Pass itself.

Snake Pass is in the Peak District in Derbyshire. It crosses the Pennines between Glossop and the Ladybower Reservoir at Ashopton. The road was built by Thomas Telford and was opened in 1821 and cost £18,625 at the time. The road has a horrendous accident record compared with other roads in the country. Go on a casual drive down one of its sections at any time of year, and you will witness crashed-down walls and the strewn remnants of wreckage from countless vehicles lining its edges. It's often closed in winter because of the weather, which includes white-outs from severe blizzards. When the rain comes for longer periods, it can result in serious subsidence which can shut the route for weeks while extensive repairs are carried out.

One of the most dangerous places on the pass is at its summit where it climbs up to meet the moorland plateaus of

Kinder Scout and Bleaklow. Here it reaches a height of 1,680 feet above sea level, and it's often shrouded in cloud and mist.

The road gets its name from the emblem of the Snake Inn, a pub on the Sheffield side of the pass and is one of the few buildings on the road. The winding nature of the route certainly lives up to its name with incredibly tight bends and rodeo-style dips and climbs. And like a lot of snakes, the road is not something to be trifled with. With this blend of bisecting terrain and bad weather, it can give a nasty bite, and in some cases, easily lead to death.

Inside the Micra, Fiona and her brother were getting restless, and as can happen with young children, they'd started to argue. This was quickly dealt with by the sharp tongue of their mother. It was odd to observe these outbursts as she yelled at her kids. She seemed less like a loving parent, and more like a prison warder at a riot with her raised tones and inferred threats. There was absolutely no love in her interactions at all. It was almost as if these were somebody else's children she'd been lumbered with, and all she wanted was them gone.

"Shall we put the radio on?" Eve suggested, trying to find solutions to the unpleasant situation. "That might occupy them a little."

"No," Deborah declared, instantly dismissing her. "This is Christmas, and we should be able to talk to each other."

And so, in the middle of this rather strange mobile, Victorian ideal Deborah had created, the muteness and hostility descended once again. It was like driving inside a freezer. The atmosphere was horrific and like something you might find on the surface of Mars. Fiona was the first to challenge the misery.

"It's snowing!" she yelled excitedly, as she watched the first of the meagre flakes slide down the outside of her window. Her grandmother turned around to face her.

"They look lovely, don't they?" she asked calmly, and then looked at her daughter. "But that could be a problem for where we're heading," she stated. "I think we should turn back."

Deborah's face turned instantly to thunder.

"It's just a bit of snow!" she barked. "Stop overreacting, will you."

"Not at the tops, it won't be. The higher we go, the colder it will become, and so there'll be ice too."

Deborah whipped her head so sharply around to confront her mother that there should have been a 'crack'.

"I'm not coming all the way over here just to turn back now!" she screamed, her words bouncing off the interior of the car like a rifle shot. Her mother ignored her and carried on.

"It's just a get-together, Deborah. Is it *really* worth the risk?"

Still facing her and seemingly not caring that she was no longer looking where she was driving, Deborah replied.

"We're going!" she decreed tersely with an assumed authority.

Over in Sheffield, things were moving on apace. Abigail had lit a huge, welcoming fire in the main reception room and whiffs of its smoke fused with the scent of the expensive candles that adorned the fine oak mantelpiece. She'd tidied the magnificent trimmings too, and the tree was like something you might have found in a public place, like a park or shopping mall, such was its size.

The snow was falling here too, only heavier. It would be, however, as this location was closer to the advancing front. Abigail peeked out through the luxuriant lounge curtains to the wide street beyond. She measured the intensity of the fall by the number of flakes which passed in front of the street lamp outside, and they were now flowing like a little river.

"Surely Deborah won't try and come over in this," she
mused with a tone of incredulity in her voice. "I hope she stays
at home like I told her to."

Her husband nudged in behind her, wearing his cosy
reindeer-encrusted, shiny jumper. He placed his head tenderly
next to his wife's as he gazed into the increasingly wild weather
outside.

"Yes, but you know what she can be like," he said.

Deborah and her party finally reached the bottom of the Snake
Pass, after prising their way through the congested traffic in
Glossop. This was half-a-town, half-a-village, with one main
road barging its way through its centre. On either side of this
artery were old-fashioned shops, which still retained their own
identities and charm. It gave the impression that it was a
friendly place where the residents looked out for each other. It
had a certain considerate vibe.

As the road cleared the houses, the lower slopes of the
moors began to take over. Gone were the neat lawns,
monuments and council flower borders. Now all that lay ahead
was relative wilderness. Deborah trundled the car nervously
along, her eyes occasionally peeking up through the upper
section of the windscreen to the heights above. The rising hills
glared down on them like towering ogres with clubs in their
hands and menace in their faces. Eve looked about her
suspiciously.

"There's hardly any cars," she pondered, "In fact, there's no
cars at all." And then she spotted something; a smallish, yellow,
stand-up sign with black writing plonked obstructively in the
middle of the road some two hundred metres away. Deborah
pulled up carefully in front of it. 'Road Ahead Closed', it read.

After barely digesting the sign's words, Deborah swiftly
revved the car's engine, found first gear, drove around it and
carried on her way up the road once more.

"What are you doing?" Eve demanded, raising her voice.

"Driving," Deborah answered, sarcastically.

"But the road's closed."

"Well, perhaps it shouldn't be. Anyone can see its fine. It's only a bit of snow, for God's sake."

"The sign's telling you that it's closed, Deborah."

Deborah brought the car to a halt suddenly, and she faced her mother.

"If you don't want to come with us, you can get out here," she suggested angrily. The car engine ticked over patiently as the air thickened with tension once again. Eve didn't reply; rather her face creased up with fury.

"Thank you," Deborah mumbled, and the car's wheels spun slightly as she set off once more leaving the sign behind them.

Over on the Sheffield side of the pass, the snow plough continued to chug its way along. Its wheels cut two furrows under its chained tyres. The huge, metal scoop on its front skimmed the first real accumulations aside like a new razor cutting through three-day-old stubble. There was no way this was the worst snow the machine or its operators had seen, but the scenario they found themselves in today was oddly different somehow – mainly because the plough was actually skidding. But this wasn't because of the covering of snow under its wheels, but because of the over-abundant ice.

The temperature had now fallen drastically as the Russian front began to connect squarely with the meek, temperate competitor ahead of it. The mercury was reading -3 degrees centigrade, and this was continuing to drop. Anything that contained water was fair game and was instantaneously transformed: the drips forming icicles on the fences; the leaves becoming paper on the trees; the surface of the road itself. Given this phenomenon, any measures the authorities had put in place to remedy the situation would become increasingly futile. Road salt would be as effective as water from a hosepipe sprayed on to lava spewing from an active volcano. Nothing would stop its advance on to the hapless town below. As the plough finally began to totally lose its grip, there would be nothing more they could do. And as the front took over this face of the hill, and then descended to its other side, the whole area would eventually be overrun.

On the climb up to the summit from the Glossop side, Deborah was leaning harder in towards the windscreen to maximise her view of the road as they began to negotiate the tight bends which cut through the lower slopes. Once clear of those, the road opened up to more of a straight climb, and with this new-found freedom in sight, Deborah smiled and put her foot down harder on the accelerator.

"See," she rejoiced smugly, "there's nothing wrong with this road. I've got through these bends with no trouble at all."

Eve finally awoke from her silence.

"They wouldn't just put up Road Closed signs for nothing, would they?" she commented. "And I really don't think you've got the car for it if we do hit problems. You need something with four-wheel drive up here – if you're up here at all." She almost pleaded with her daughter now. "Can we not just turn back while we still can?"

"We'll be all right," Deborah dismissed her. "I'm not being late, and that's that. Why don't you read a magazine or something?"

"You've got children in the car, Fiona!"

"You can see all the way up to the top. There's hardly any snow there or anything."

"You should still trust whoever put that sign out. I'm telling you; we should turn back now."

"And I'm telling you; we'll be fine!" Deborah's eyes suddenly darkened as one of her rages instantly took over her. "Just fucking shut up, mother, will you!" she bawled.

In the salubrious suburb in Sheffield, Abigail was looking more and more concerned. She left her preparations in the kitchen, hurried into the lounge and hunted down her mobile phone. Her husband watched her pick it up from the arm of the sofa and then hastily search out a name on her contact list.

"Deborah?" he asked quizzically. Abigail nodded as she listened intently as her call rang out and then connected with Deborah's voicemail.

"I think she's turned it off," Abigail revealed, sounding worried. "I hope to God she's not on her way."

The driver of the snow plough had finally given up his attempt to climb any further up the hill, so he reversed the machine slowly back down following in the tracks he'd laid earlier. The section of the sky directly above them now had an odd, pink shade about it. A massive cavern had formed in the clouds, and it looked weird and intimidating. At the highest part, wispy, thin clouds streaked its roof resembling trails of liquid oxygen. It was almost possible to pick out the frozen particles extending from them and they looked like long braids of petrified white hair.

The driver of the plough now stopped his machine, and the crew with him began chipping at the road with the metal caps of their boots. The frequency of their strikes seemed to suggest that they were trying to break through something but were failing to do so. One of them bent down to get a closer look at this new impenetrable layer of ice, which now covered the road like additional, prohibiting, transparent tarmacadam. Then one of them pointed up to the area of sky behind them all. A huge roll of grey-black clouds was approaching, and as the men saw it, they immediately headed straight to their nearby Range Rovers, only stopping to erect two more 'Road Closed' signs before they boarded them and hurriedly left.

In the mighty Micra, Deborah's shouts rattled around the cabin as she celebrated.

"We're almost there, we're almost there!" she whooped, as the summit loomed into sight. The pass had levelled significantly now, and it just needed a kink left, and one right again, and then a skip over a small bridge before it reached the top of the hill. Beyond the summit the road would fall again; it would tumble rapidly, forming the steepest part of the route. From here the pass sped on towards Sheffield, hugging the side of a narrow valley. To the right of the road, a precipitous drop appeared, which had swallowed up many a vehicle and its occupants over the years. It sat there like the waiting, gaping jaws of a huge, hungry crocodile.

"You see," Deborah chirped as she picked out the still relatively tame flurries of snow through the windscreen. "I said there'd be no snow – and I was right!" She smirked again as the car weaved slightly just as they approached the very peak of the hill. And then Eve let out a blood-curdling scream.

"Stop!"

She bellowed so loudly she frightened everyone.

"Mummy!" Fiona yelped, terrified by her cry.

Deborah's eyes flashed quickly to her mother. "What the hell is wrong with you!" she yelled in turn.

"I said, stop!" Eve repeated, ignoring her vitriolic words.

Deborah carried on driving regardless. "I'm not stopping. Why should I stop?" she retorted. "We're virtually there."

And then as the car tipped over the brow of the hill, Deborah spotted something.

"Oh my God!" she roared, and she stamped on the brakes as hard as she could. The car obligingly stopped initially, but then it began to slide forwards of its own accord on the thick carpet of ice that was now under its wheels.

"Shit," Deborah squealed. "Fucking shit!"

The descending pass looked like the surface of a glacier. Further down the hill, there were dozens of cars which had simply been left where they'd stopped, their drivers giving up their meaningless attempts to climb any higher. As they'd connected with the ice, all traction had been lost, and the vehicles had slid backwards and ended up crashing into walls, fences, rocks – and each other. One had even fallen into the valley itself, and it was now perched on the top of a cliff halfway down, its front wheels dangling over the edge like the legs of bather at a pool on a hot, steamy summer's afternoon.

But what made this scene scariest of all was the fact that the whole place was deserted. But it more than likely would be. After all, the emergency services would be working on the logic that no one would be stupid enough to bypass the signs they'd purposely set out on the approaches down near Glossop. All the radio stations had been broadcasting warnings for the last four hours, and because Deborah was too engrossed in haranguing her kids, she'd missed the illuminated sign in the centre of the town telling her that the pass was closed.

"Well, do something!" Eve shrieked at her daughter, but Deborah just sat there paralysed as the car continued to slide. Seeing this, Eve grabbed the wheel and pulled against Deborah's grip and the car rolled slowly into the kerb where the road met the edges of the moor, and it held there, but only just, threatening to career off down the hill at any moment.

Deborah was now an utterly different person – but not necessarily for the better. A panic took over her, and she began to whimper.

"What are we going to do?" she bleated pathetically. "What are we going to do?" Fiona and George began to cry too, but perhaps understandably so after having been gifted with all this terror so unexpectedly.

Eve turned to the children first and gave them a reassuring smile. Then she carefully took Fiona's hand.

"Fiona?" she began, hardly making herself heard above Deborah's sobbing. "Could you do something for me?" she asked calmly. Fiona nodded through her tears, her fear making her hiccup now. "Good," Eve smiled. "I need you to stop crying." Eve looked at George. "And you too, George," she went on. "Can you do that for me?"

Fiona reached over and seized her brother's hand and squeezed it softly.

"We have to help Nana now," she said to him. The soothing feel to her voice seemed to help George, and his crying began to lessen. "That's better," Fiona praised him gently, stroking his hair as she did so, and after a few moments, he'd stopped altogether.

"You're both being very brave," Eve complimented them and then she turned to face her daughter.

"And now you need to be brave too, love," she encouraged her tenderly, and she leaned over and kissed Deborah on her cheek and wiped away her tears. Eve seemed to realise that Deborah could so easily be disabled by her own fear; the way mice are when they're cornered in the tank of a hungry snake, waiting for the strike.

Fiona watched as her grandmother took control of the situation without waiting for any more permissions or arguments. But she didn't do this by threatening or bullying, but by remaining composed, being strong, giving reasons why something needed doing – and only then directing actions rather than ordering them to happen.

"This car is heavy," Eve explained, addressing all of them, holding her daughter's hand. Deborah's sobbing had evolved into a long, low repetitive moan. "The heavier it is," Eve continued, "the more it wants to go forwards, and we don't want that. So what we need to do is reduce that weight. And the best way to do that is for you, Fiona, George and your mummy to get *carefully* and *slowly* out of the car. Once you've done that, then I can try and drive the car back up the hill."

"But it's cold outside," Deborah protested weakly, sounding like a little girl again.

"I know it is, love," Eve answered her softly. "But it'll only be for a little while, and once we're back at the top of the hill and on the road again, you can get back in. We've got plenty of petrol, the engine's still running fine, and it'll get warm again in here in no time."

Deborah looked at her mother in a way that she hadn't done for many years.

"Promise?" she asked. Deborah needed her now, like the times a daughter really needs their mother; when their strength has gone, when they discover that we are all still extremely vulnerable.

"I promise," Eve replied. "Come on; we're going to be okay."

And that's what they did. Fiona was the first to move. It was as if they were now all sitting on a pile of dynamite. She opened her door slowly and led her brother out, popping up the hood on his parka before the cold hit him. She gently closed the door and walked around the body of the car until she reached the driver's door. Once there she creaked it open and took her mother's hand.

"Come on, Mummy," she coaxed, "it's really not that bad."

Once they'd exited the car, Eve let herself out.

"I'll see you at the top," she said cheerily as Fiona led the rest of their party skilfully away.

Once they were gone, Eve went to the left front wheel and oddly began to let air out of the tyre. The valve hissed, and with the tyre now a third deflated, she did the same on the other front wheel. She'd explain to everyone later that doing this increased the amount of rubber that made contact with the road and so effectively improved the tyre's grip. Then she climbed into the driver's seat and after waiting for Fiona and her two charges to clear her way, she put the car into reverse, slowly revved the engine and let the clutch connect evenly with the transmission. Bit by bit, the car began to nudge up the hill, half of it now running on the heather and moss rather than on the hard surface of the road itself.

After two minutes, the plucky little Nissan passed by the apex of the summit. Once there, Eve turned the car around with minute zig-zags, so it was facing towards Glossop again. Soon Fiona, her brother and her mother were back in the car warming up. Eve found the foot pump in the boot and re-inflated the tyres. Once done, she replaced it in its carrier and then sat back in the driver's seat once more.

"Everybody fine?" she asked considerately, still sounding remarkably unflustered. Fiona nodded. Eve smiled at her grandson. "George?" He smiled back and then Eve turned to her daughter. "And what about you, love?" she queried gently. Deborah's eyes filled with tears again suddenly and she began to cry.

"I'm ... sorry," she howled uncontrollably. Eve seized her hand.

"It's all right," she assured her, forgiveness already present in her eyes. "We're all going to be all right."

Eve found first gear and drove as fast as she possibly dared as the snowfall began to build. She glimpsed in the mirror and watched the rear window as it began to be covered by a thickening, white layer. She checked her daughter to see how she was. Deborah was looking down into the footwell of the passenger seat. She hardly moved. Her face was white and gaunt, etched with two lines of thick, unattended-to mascara.

After twenty minutes of tracking the road along its centre, they eventually made it back down to the lower slopes. Fiona looked back up the road through her side window as they negotiated one of the last sharp bends, and she seemed amazed to see that theirs were the only tracks riding on the back of the pass now. When they entered Glossop, Eve found a safe place to pull in. She took out her mobile phone and dialled a number. A phone rang, and someone quickly answered.

"Hi, Abigail, it's Mum," Eve announced. "I'm with Deborah. I'm afraid we won't be coming over today," she said.

CHAPTER EIGHTEEN

The building seemed out of place. It was situated just on the
outskirts of the county town, which wasn't terribly big, and so it
seemed too large; like a massive head on top of a tiny body. It
was a conglomeration of huge concrete squares piled on top of
each other, and when they couldn't go any higher, they simply
oozed out sideways occupying even more land. To complete
the overburdening picture, the Crown Court was here too, and
this relatively minute community would see trials for serious
crimes, which were way beyond anything it experienced locally.
Murderers and bank robbers were transported to the rear
entrance of the structure in bulletproof vans accompanied by
armed guards. It was like something out of the Wild West. But
as well as being inconvenienced with this disproportionate
spectacle, the town was the designated political centre for the
county too. Here policies were thrashed out and decisions made
for the whole region. It was the home of the county council
and there was a full meeting of it today, in the chambers
incorporated within the giant building.

The first of the cars arrived as the members of the council
began to trickle in for the 10 am start. The car park was large
and accommodating, but some of the drivers seemed to be
struggling with the bays. A number were turning a simple task
into something clumsy and tedious, as they appeared unable to
work out angles properly, holding up the flow of traffic as they
dithered around. There was a total lack of any proficiency

displayed in their behaviour as they did this – nothing efficient, challenging or effective. Everything was transformed into a grinding, dismal dullness.

A steady stream of councillors eventually entered the building. Here, most of them were recognised, and they were greeted like royalty by the staff at the broad reception desk. Section by section, they were ushered into a large, official chamber which had an oversized chair raised on a plinth at one end. It looked quite surreal standing there on its own, like some odd prop out of an *Alice in Wonderland* set. This is where the head of the council would sit in official ceremonies, lording it over all the lesser beings assembled before him. It was a throne where people were gifted with authority rather than having to earn it. Five minutes of meandering later; finding the right seat, chatting about tittle-tattle, posturing and strutting, and they were all finally settled.

The chairman was a man in his mid-sixties. He was small and skinny with patchy, greying, bizarre hair. Big tufts of it were missing, and it gave the impression that his head had been on fire.

The agendas were laid out around the massive table. They were meticulously positioned individually by each member, and the chair allowed all those present to take a moment to study them. There were over forty people at this well-attended quarterly affair.

"Ladies and Gentlemen," the chairman began, "you'll find all the items for the meeting in the packs in front of you. There is just one last-minute entry, which has been added since the documents were printed, and I would draw your attention to that." He looked down through his glasses as he rippled the wedge of pages he grasped in his wrinkled hands, which trembled ever so slightly. "It's on page seven," he explained, and looked up at the big oval of people gathered around the table ahead of him before carrying on.

"Given recent events, it's something that's been hastily drawn up by our legal and estates teams," he elucidated. He paused for a moment. "It's a proposal forbidding entry to any person other than a council official to the entire site of what is colloquially known as the 'Incident Pit'". He scanned the attentive faces as if he was waiting for some kind of negative reaction, but there was none. He looked pleased. "We'll be looking to get approval for this proposal and to annexe its recommendations to the by-laws at today's meeting if we can, fellow Members of the Council," he advised them all austerely.

CHAPTER NINETEEN

He seemed eerily at home at this depth. He would have appeared calm through his mask; if anyone had been there to see him. But this was one of his strengths. The tougher things turned, the more relaxed and capable he seemed to become. It was like blind panic but in reverse. It was a truly enviable quality. And he'd need that composure now, there in that totally exclusive environment, in the near-blackness; a torch Martin's only aid in this bat-like world.

He bobbed ever so slightly as he looked around him, taking his time not to make any sudden movements, planning every action because of the possibility of its consequences; gear dropped, his mask dislodged; something cataclysmic, given where he was.

"So, here we are again," Martin announced with a mix of solemnity and humour, "me under the water on the mic, me on my own once more. But the place wasn't exactly buzzing with offers, was it?"

Fiona, Phil and John were all huddled around a table in the middle of the main room in the clubhouse. The same equipment that Martin had used before was there, assembled on its top. They all looked a little guilty at hearing Martin's last words, and they looked concerned too. But as their friend had pointed out; he hadn't asked anyone to attend his next attempt. "This show will run itself," he'd said. "No one actually needs to be here." He'd gone on to say that he'd only told them he was trying for the record again – albeit at the last minute, because they would have tried to stop him – because it wasn't fair to inflict all 'that secrecy' on everyone for another time. Besides, as he'd concluded, they'd probably have found out about it for themselves anyway. So why not just be honest about the whole thing?

Martin's voice squealed out through the speaker again.

"Maybe I'm cursed or something," he resumed with a slight chuckle. "Some bloke off *Pirates of the Caribbean* with tentacles and jellyfish sticking out of his face, spending the rest of eternity in some beat-up old boat with a bunch of smelly twats with no teeth and cannonball holes through their heads." Then he was more serious. "Yeah, and I've already done that one: why don't I just wait until I'm fully recovered, until things are just right again? Thing is, time ain't my shipmate at the moment, my old muckers. Call me paranoid, but I've heard they're coming, that those guys from Stoney are actually on their way. I couldn't bear someone else beating me to it, not after everything that's happened. And that's before those wankers at the council close it down for good. I know they're only rumours, but they're close enough for me. Anyway; so, here I am. The data and images should be rolling down your screen as we speak; something for the record books, and if not that, posterity, eh?"

Phil shook his head slowly, focusing on the speaker, as if he might get extra meaning or understanding from the situation by looking at it so intensely.

"I'm at one hundred and twenty-five metres now," Martin carried on.

Phil's eyes skipped immediately sideways to the laptop which confirmed Martin's information by displaying a large '125m' on its screen.

"My air's better this time," Martin resumed, "and I've got eyes on absolutely every-thing. Still bloody cold though."

Fiona looked at the floor again, a thicker veil of worry now evident on her face.

"This is the deepest I've ever been," Martin began once more, "so if something's going to pop, blow or fuck up, now's its chance. It really *is* incredible down here though. Everybody should be made to come."

John looked at his companions in turn. His eyes bore a kind of jealousy. Then Martin spoke again.

"God, that hurts," he exclaimed. All three of his observers suddenly leaned closer to the speaker.

"Shit," Phil hissed.

"Chest's become suddenly tight," Martin struggled on. They heard him cough. "That doesn't feel good," Martin wheezed. "Shit. That doesn't feel good at all."

Phil swept up the mic suddenly into his grasping hand.

"Martin? Martin! Are you all right?"

There was no answer; simply interference through the radio which sounded like millions of eggs frying.

"Martin!"

"Fuck. He's in trouble!" John cried.

Fiona put her head in her hands. "Jesus, why wouldn't he listen! Why does he have to do these things?" she bawled.

Then there was a silence when no one said anything. After ten more seconds the sound of Martin's voice finally drifted through the speaker. It was suddenly lighter, its humour having returned, but with that, there was a brave acceptance that something awful was about to happen.

"Hey, Rob. One last raz on the Busa, eh?" he said.

CHAPTER TWENTY

The man standing in front of him suddenly turned and fled. It was as if a young deer had suddenly worked out that the creature it had been so inquisitive about was actually a lion, and having suddenly realised that, now was the time act, to save itself. Martin did his best to catch him up, as the man navigated his way deftly past the drunken people who were lining the walls of the hall, past the cooing couple in the kitchen, and out into the back garden and the exit to the street beyond. Martin gave up the chase by the kitchen door and watched him go. The man from the couple looked aggressively over at him.

"What's wrong with *him*?" Martin commented to anyone who might be listening, slurring his words and nodding in the direction of the recently departed escapee. The glass in his hand was still remarkably well charged despite all the commotion he was creating. And then another gormless grin, and Martin reversed out of the room, careful of his footing. It was as if he was some semi-truck stuck with its nose down the wrong way of a narrow alley and every movement was necessarily short and cumbersome.

He moved on to the lounge where the music was blasting from next and looked creepily around for another victim. And soon he found one. Bev from marketing was always an easy target for anyone to plant a one-sided conversation upon. She spent a great deal of time on her own and seemed to readily accept the imposition. She was brilliant at her job, especially with anything that was written down, but socialising was still something she needed to work at. Martin obviously knew this, and he wallowed over to pincer her at their boss's fiftieth birthday celebration being held here in his large and vulgar house. Bev resembled a cornered animal now and Martin started up again like a choky old engine, not waiting to be invited to speak.

"Now you," he began to roll, beaming at her stupidly, "you're not competitive – but me!" Martin staggered slightly, and Bev took half a precautionary step backwards. "Well, you know me, don't you? But that's not my fault, you see," he persisted. She took another step. "Hey, no. Don't go!" he shouted and reached out to her as she began to run. As she scrambled out by the far end of the lounge, Martin skulked around on the spot – only now looking decidedly humiliated. A few awkward seconds ticked by. "Bleedin' office party things," he moaned.

But then he noticed a couple sitting at the table in the corner, who'd been talking quietly before he'd followed Bev in. Martin appeared instantly pleased that they were there. It was almost as if he'd already calculated how difficult it would be for them to get away from him and he sidled up and faced them squarely, setting them in his sights. He wore a boastful smile of delight as he did so.

"I blame *that* little bastard personally," Martin launched off brutally, and his face turned suddenly bitter as he approached closer, now boxing them in. "I was always the second favourite in my parents' eyes. RAF, he was, some 'star'," he rumbled on. The couple exchanged a quick glance. "Ended up as a wing commander when he was barely out of puberty." Martin smiled. "The closest thing I've ever been to a 'wing commander' is when I've been in KFC gorging over the barbeque ones after a particularly heavy night on the piss, out in town. Everywhere we went; 'Alexander this, Alexander-fucking-that'. That's why I do the diving, see; nothing to do with them. They'd only dismiss it anyway."

The couple passed another look between them, silently planning their route clear of the situation. Martin countered simply with a pace forwards and a point of his finger that brandished more than a degree of threat.

"They could never quite grasp why I wanted to dive and so, thankfully, they left me alone," he continued, blissfully disregarding their indisputable intentions. "I hardly ever see them now." He looked down at the floor in a sporadic moment of contemplation accompanied by a more than ample portion of self-pity. "My dad's not that well. My mother's still a snooty cow but, you know; now I just can't be arsed. And my spoilt, perfect, little brother?" He raised his head angrily. "Well, he can just go and fuck himself! I've grown tired of them. Hurt me too much, see."

The girl in the couple reached out for and found her partner's hand as Martin took a minor break in his rant. "Have they any idea of how hard it was for a kid like me to fight for his place in normal life without them all being total wankers as well?" he resumed. "They never forgave me for having dyslexia. I don't think they thought it was a real thing. They always treated me like I was 'handicapped' or something. Suppose I was in a way, but why should that matter? The word I could always spell right was 'dickheads' though – I made a special effort just for them!"

Suddenly the man nodded to the girl as if they'd finally agreed their plan.

"I won't see any of them *ever* again," Martin wailed, as if people were compelled to listen to his words. "Sad, really that, isn't it?" He grinned, almost evilly. "But I've found my own world to go to without them, with my own hell-bent challenges to take on. I can be a 'commander' too. All those wonderful places down there, things to discover – without them!" Martin turned strangely to one side now facing slightly away from the couple, as if he was relishing his next words ahead of uttering them. "My new kingdom that they can never, ever, *ever* get to," he proclaimed.

Then in one unified movement, the couple rose from the table. Rather cleverly, they split, heading off in different directions, leaving Martin's head spinning, unsure of whom to track. Eventually, he settled on the girl.

"Hey, don't go. Don't you go too!" he called after her miserably, his arms open wide. "Stay, eh?" he bleated on, pivoting round to focus on the man, this other refugee from their dreadful, incarcerating conversation. "Look, you know what I'm like when I've had few." He beckoned him back towards him. "Don't go! Stay. Please!" Martin stretched out his hand as if trying to seize hold of the disappearing figure by his collar. "Just stay … hey?"

As he watched the man finally exit the room, Martin lowered his arm slowly, and after a few seconds he let out a long and painful sigh. "Stay," he groaned.

CHAPTER TWENTY-ONE

It was quite surreal; the group of three in their inflatable, mid-water in the Pit, waiting for Martin to pop up through the surface of the water – as if they were whale-watching, the anticipation and tension building. It was as if an orca might suddenly rise out clear and then breach at any moment. There was no giant mammal, however, only Martin, and he appeared a few moments later. He shot out of the water like a missile and then landed again with an impressive splash, his life-saver now fully inflated, the bends already having wrecked his body.

They wrestled him into the boat. There were no words of panic. It was as if the three of them weren't surprised by what they'd found. It was like sifting through the bargain bin in a supermarket where all the about-to-be-out-of-date items are placed. It's not that surprising to find something that's been damaged lying there.

On their way back to shore, John took out his mobile phone and called for an ambulance. There was an odd gap in the call-handler's response after he gave their location. It was like a part in a conversation where a killer-bee keeper is asking for a life insurance quote, and there's a predictable silence.

Phil nestled the boat into the little cove with its small jetty, and they carefully laid Martin on the grassiest bank they could find among the jagged edges of the slate. Then Fiona moved to Martin's side as John and Phil took a step back. They were all still remarkably calm. They suspected that Martin was beyond medical help. They watched as Martin finally gained consciousness, the odd recollections now finally leaving him like troublesome hotel guests he'd finally managed to evict. He'd find it partly amusing and partly annoying that his mind hadn't been occupied, as it's supposed to be in situations like these, by key images of his life flashing before his eyes, but rather by a re-run of a more mundane, degrading and painful experience.

He scanned around, disorientated at first, and then his eyes fixed on Fiona's face. He seemed relieved to see her as she smiled kindly down at him.

"We think you've had a heart attack, Martin," she informed him almost casually, her tone quiet and considerate. Martin took a moment to respond as he digested her comment and then he forced out a mutinous smile.

"Well, I've been trying hard enough for one, haven't I?" he jibed, obviously in pain, obviously struggling. "Glad not to disappoint, eh?"

A few moments passed in which neither of them said anything. They both seemed to be fully absorbing the severity of the situation they'd found themselves in.

"Happy now?" Fiona asked eventually, sadly, tears welling in her eyes. Martin grinned, some of his bloodied teeth showing through his ravaged lips.

"Well apart from the fact that I've got a thistle sticking in my arse, I'm perfectly fine, thanks," he quipped. Fiona's voice was still soft.

"So now you've taken kamikaze to a completely different level," she said.

"Well, at least you aren't giving me a total bollocking. I should be grateful for that, I suppose," Martin retorted, still looking guilty, however.

There was another pause in their conversation. They exchanged a look between them which confirmed that it was way too late for bollockings now.

Fiona took Martin's hand. He held a look on her for a while, and then he turned his head so he could gaze at the sky. A few thick, rounded cumulus clouds were passing by. They weren't the full cotton wool type you find on a blissfully, beautiful summer's day, but they had part of that quality about them all the same. They possessed a wonderful richness, which Martin seemed to appreciate in his brief period of contemplation.

"How's the pain now?" Fiona enquired sensitively, her intonation suggesting she was dreading his answer.

Martin sounded dreamlike now.

"Imagine growing up in a world where you weren't controlled, processed, where you were free like the sea. Wouldn't that be wonderful?" he pondered.

Fiona smiled to herself. "Why do you never directly answer a question?" she asked him affectionately.

Martin hesitated and then grinned again. "Do you like salmon?" he replied obliquely.

Fiona shook her head gently in disbelief. "What?"

"Fish-farmed or free?"

"What ... does it matter?"

"To the salmon, it might. There's all that effort, swimming upstream, waterfalls, leaping about – just to end up as bear shit at the end of it all. But it spends at least some of its life doing what it wants to; being free." Martin turned to face Fiona again. "Not from a farm – that's me," he stated defiantly, fire still clearly evident in his eyes.

"Still thinking everything is just that simple?"

"It could be," Martin continued assuredly. "But when it's difficult sometimes you just do it, you know? Snow outside, got to get to work to earn a living, can't if you don't, so you find your coat, open the front door and ... brace. Soon you're in your car, engine on. The ice slips off the windscreen, and you're on your way." Even though the pain inside his body was so plainly increasing, Martin forced out another smile. "Do difficult," he almost ordered, "see the snow, brace. Open that door." Martin took Fiona's hands in his, and he held them tightly, and for a considerable while. "It feels so fantastic, having tried." And then that one last loving smile. "Take the kit down, try again; finish the job, Fiona," he said.

Martin's head fell slowly to one side. It came to rest in a shallow and comfortable hollow in the bank beneath his skull. It was as if the ground had been specifically designed for this purpose, and it looked strangely natural as the life drifted from his body. His eyes remained half open, but there was no blink.

His colour had already started to change too. The rigours of his pinkish complexion were being swapped for hints of cooler lilacs and all-consuming greys. As the muscles in his face relaxed, all expressions of pain and anxiety were gone. In their place now was this vision of peace, but of pride too. This was the look someone wears after having achieved something; the buzz after the thrill; the chance they took that they would always be remembered for. And similarly, the wearer of this expression is a person others look at with admiration and envy; wishing it was them, wondering if it could ever be, realising that probably it wouldn't be. This would be the same look others would bestow on Martin's beloved Hayabusa when he was parked outside a café somewhere. Now he and the bike would be seen as the same entity, recalled with the same spirit – and that was something he would have been so extraordinarily happy with.

"Martin!" Fiona cried, "Martin!" She placed her hands either side of his face and straightened and lifted his head so she could address him more directly. "Martin!"

Martin didn't respond, so she felt for a pulse on his neck, but there was nothing there for her to sense.

"Shit!"

She put her ear against his mouth listening for breathing, but again she heard nothing.

"Martin!"

She hastily bent down and positioned her ear hard against his chest, trying to pick up a heartbeat, but there was no sound here for her to detect. She kept her head where it was for five more seconds and then spoke her next words with dread and realisation.

"No," she murmured dismally. After a brief while, she slowly raised her head and sat straight again. She took his hand and held it fondly against her cheek. "Oh, Martin …" she sighed as the sadness tore into her and the rolling tears came.

One of them landed on Martin's face, but rather than leave it there untidying his skin, she wiped it away keeping him presentable and smart, keeping him how she'd like to remember him; unblemished, uniquely individual, and fulfilled.

CHAPTER TWENTY-TWO

"Yes, *fear* is the thing."

The SS officer savoured her taste as he stared deep into Eve's face. She turned away in disgust, like someone does when raw meat is thrust under their nose. But then she suddenly spun back around and faced him again.

"Cancers can be cut out, parasites starved or poisoned," she advised him coolly – and then spat violently into his face.

Her spittle dribbled slowly down the SS officer's cheeks as he maintained his hateful stare. Only when it reached his mouth did he finally move away and wipe it begrudgingly clear on to the sleeve of his jacket. Eve straightened herself on her chair and closed her legs as the SS officer took a moment to readjust his uniform. He nodded as he stood tall again, smiling cynically as he did so.

"The 'spirit'?" he chortled mockingly. "Some say he looks like a bulldog." His tone was riddled with insult now. "But of course, they are all still dogs," he croaked callously. Eve heretically returned his smile.

"Fear only works if you allow it to," she informed him, almost with a hint of consideration in her voice. And then her smile vanished in an instant and was replaced by an expression of pure loathing. "I have no fear of you," she continued. "When my duty is done, I will return home, enjoy this glorious life I've been given. I shall be happy. I will laugh, dance, marry and have children; grow old with them. I will teach them all I know; and above all else, I will teach them never to live in fear of tyrants in whatever form or wherever in the world they come from."

She looked skywards for a few seconds, contemplating something.

"The RAF are on their way," she said, sounding pleased as she faced the SS officer once again. "I radioed them well before you captured me. They have the coordinates for your facility," – she looked around her quickly – "here." She fixed him with a penetrating glare. "Better to be a bulldog than some other sort of animal."

The SS officer approached her again, obviously still trying to intimidate her.

"What would you suggest?" he rumbled.

"Hyena," Eve recommended. "Did you know that their call bears an uncanny resemblance to a human laugh? But they have that dreadful reputation. People see them as scavengers, cowards who would rather steal meals from more successful predators than hunt or kill their prey themselves." She thought for a moment and then looked suddenly happier, now wearing a thick expression of satisfaction. "By my calculation, the bombers should be here by now," she carried on. "Why do you think I've 'entertained' you for so long?" She grinned. "Soon you'll revert to type; you'll hide, save yourself, scurry away."

"Really? Is that what I'll do?"

Suddenly an air raid siren burst into life from one of the buildings outside. As Eve smiled rebelliously, the SS officer gazed immediately up towards the sky. Now he resembled a frightened child. He was picking at the stone and concrete above his head with his eyes, desperate to see what was beyond them.

"Odd. I don't hear you laughing," Eve commented sardonically. The SS officer was dumbstruck for a while.

"You called them in on yourself?"

"Fortune favours the bold," Eve answered him soulfully. "Or perhaps I'll just get lucky."

Now, as the growl of the approaching low-flying bombers filled the room, the SS officer skittered about trying to process the sounds he was hearing. Seeming sure he had correctly identified what they were, and without saying anything more to Eve, he turned the key in the heavy metal door and battered his way out to the open space beyond, leaving his prisoner on her own. The engines of the two Lancasters sang out in a rhythmic harmony as the aircraft got closer. After twenty more seconds, their noise reverberated off the walls. Things rattled and hummed as they were devoured by the din. Eve looked about her momentarily, scanning her surroundings. She looked convinced – but also content – that what her eyes settled on now would be the very last things she would see.

CHAPTER TWENTY-THREE

The best thing about Fiona's flat was its balcony. She could see things. In the previous property she'd rented, the closest she'd got to an unobstructed view of the sky was via its conservatory. But that had a replacement roof made of new-fangled glass, which regulated heat and allegedly cleaned itself. It was dulled as a result, and it was like looking at everything through several pairs of sunglasses. But being here at her new place, meant that Fiona could see the moon and stars with ease, and she'd spend hours on her new perch trussed up in her dressing gown, wearing her beanie hat, staring contently up at them. She'd been doing this tonight. She was still trying to make sense of things, to find reasons, a way forwards, strength; hope possibly.

"Why was it so easy for you?" Fiona asked out loud, seemingly not caring if anyone was looking in on her and what they might make of her talking to herself if they were. She picked out a particularly bright star and focused on it. "I mean, I know you weren't religious or anything like that, you had no *secret formula* as far as I know. So what was it? Why were you *so* strong?"

She broke her gaze from the universe and looked down again as she recalled something and smiled.

"I can never remember seeing you stressed. Maybe it was because of what you'd been through. Maybe you were tested beyond the limits any normal person could comprehend. An elastic band, stretched, and if elasticity is stress, worry, 'disstress', then yours was gone for ever, wasn't it?" Fiona's expression changed. There was almost a layer of bitterness on her face now. "I wish I was more like you!" she cried.

She stood and wandered around the space for a while. She checked the leaves on one of her plants that was lined up with others on the floor against the bright, white wall. She peered down on to the gardens of the lines of houses below with their predominantly tidy lawns, neat hedges and variety of competing summerhouses. The closest to her had frills on the edges of its roof, and it looked slightly silly as it nestled there in one corner of its plot.

"I've tried to fight this bloody … fear," she carried on, now sounding anxious. "But I still can't. It's come out of the shadows, materialised, taken form and, now it's wrapped around me like some huge, slithering … python; constricting, gripping me tighter and tighter, the inevitable already clearly in sight." She lowered her head as a realisation seemed to pummel her. "It's crushing the very life out of me," she whimpered, and then looked at her star again suddenly. "So, Nana, my dear, *sweet* Nana, please tell me; what should I do?"

Fiona made her way back to her chair, dallying now, as if she'd instantly acquired an extra fifty years. Just for a moment, her balcony resembled the lounge of an old people's home where the residents go to squander away the remaining hours of their days. She found the stout arms and lowered herself back into the inviting, attractive, floral cushion and let out one of those sighs that just seem to come out of nowhere.

"Ah …" she said as she exhaled.

After a few moments, she touched the outside of her dressing-gown pocket, feeling for something. The pocket was deep and safe, and she seemed relieved that an object was still present inside it. Slowly she drew it out. She held it delicately in her hand, taking care not to finger-mark its shiny surfaces. She nodded acceptingly, almost as if she'd placed it there earlier in the expectation that she might need it at some point later, following some decision or other. Her expression suggested that a particular decision had now been made.

"You always said I might need this someday," she recounted affectionately as she stared at the CD. She smiled slightly. "I just thought you were being my 'elderly relative' or something when you handed it to me; something I shouldn't pay too much attention to, ignore maybe. And then you said those words: 'Something from a different age made fresh again by need'."

Fiona moved slowly to a portable CD player which sat on top of a cute, low, wooden table over by the opposite wall. After switching it on, she placed the disc on the drawer, which had obligingly opened. She stood patiently as it played. After fifteen seconds, the history-crackled voice of Winston Churchill boomed out filling the air around her.

We shall go on to the end. We shall fight in France. We shall fight on the seas and oceans. We shall fight with growing confidence and growing strength in the air. We shall defend our island whatever the cost may be. We shall fight on the beaches. We shall fight on the landing grounds. We shall fight in the fields and in the streets. We shall fight in the hills. We shall NEVER surrender.

Fiona reached down and tapped the 'Stop' button on the player, and the sound ceased. Then she took the CD out and placed it tenderly but determinedly back in her warm pocket as if it wouldn't be needed to be played again. She moved back to her chair and sat once more. She looked different now, more sure of things; resolved even. After a few moments, she calmly resumed her musing up at the stars, still looking grateful that she no longer had to battle against the infuriating opacity of her new conservatory roof.

CHAPTER TWENTY-FOUR

What struck customers the most was how clean this restaurant was. And then they were mesmerised by its true splendour, occupying as it did a good one hundred metres of the harbour front in Mahon. This was prime real estate, with this part of Menorca commanding extraordinary values. Any business here had to do well to pay its levies and taxes, but Restaurant Jules did, and impressively so.

It had been established by an ex-pat from Britain five years previously, and now it was the envy of its neighbours who lined this stretch. Prior booking was essential, their website boasted, and consequently, prices were high. It hadn't always been this popular, however. The restaurant was only as it was now because the owner took a risk. He'd discovered it as a half-derelict, run down place that could so easily have been demolished. He had a vision no one else could see. He'd decided to move away from England, and on one of his visits over to find premises, he'd stumbled into a chance meeting with a brilliant but disgruntled chef from a nearby bistro, and fate had intervened.

The owner was sitting outside at one of the long line of tables that graced the immaculately scrubbed terrace overlooking the moorings. Here there were ships rather than boats; such were their size and quality. Many were worth several millions, and most had their own crews, uniformed and polite, who served their captains well on these floating castles.

The owner of Jules was in his mid-fifties, and he always took time to break away from the rigours of his business at this time of day. At 10.30 am every morning he'd be there, enjoying half-an-hour in the open air before the sun got too unbearable. He'd spend this time relaxing with a fine cup of coffee made by the restaurant's very own barista. He'd watch the world go by or catch up on what was happening in the world. He was doing this now when one of the waiters approached him. The waiter was beautifully dressed and groomed. He looked more like a model than someone who served in a restaurant, albeit one of the best in the Mediterranean.

"You have some mail, Mister Carter," he announced helpfully in his thick Spanish accent. It was evident that he liked the man he was addressing, his face already creased up with affection before he spoke. The restaurant owner smiled gratefully back at him.

"Thank you, Carlos," he acknowledged. "But you didn't need to bring it out; I could have collected it from the office."

Carlos shook his head ever so slightly as he handed over the bundle of letters.

"It's no problem. Anything for the boss, hey?" he said, laughing lightly now, giving a little bow before he turned and left.

Mark Carter scanned quickly through the letters and, seeing nothing of urgency or interest, he placed them down on the table in front of him. He picked up his mobile phone and continued flipping through the news pages. Three scrolls in and he froze. He moved his chair back a little as if he now needed more space. He sat more upright, re-examining what he was reading as if he wanted to make sure that what he was seeing was actually there. Deciding that it was, he peered gingerly at the headline which read: 'Incident Pit Claims Another Life.'

Below the headline was a picture of Martin. Mark placed his phone carefully and slowly back on the table. He was clearly in a state of shock. He turned to the harbour, looking out past the armada in front of him to the sea beyond, and his eyes filled with tears as he recalled a memory.

This place was once a market town, but during the industrial revolution, the mining of coal changed virtually everything. Most of the location became angular and cold. Charmless brick replaced graceful stone and wood, and the area became an exemplar of the featureless and boring. The coal didn't last, however, and when the seams were exhausted, the town remained in its altered state. Given the labour force the industry had once needed, it still housed thousands of people. Anyone born here became an unwilling prisoner in this isolated outpost. New trades and businesses appeared, and there were several government initiatives put in place to prop up the economy. People still had to buy things to survive, so some commerce thrived – but much did not. So why one shop owner had decided to open a high-end, specialist hi-fi and audio outfit right in the middle of the high street was particularly baffling.

It was a classic example of someone's passion getting the better of their reasoning. When this happens, these people misguidedly believe that everyone else has their obsession too and that, rather dangerously, this might translate into sales. For AVS, this clearly wasn't the case. The shop saw minute numbers of customers coming through its doors, and most of those who did venture in could never have afforded the prices. Before too long the business was in serious trouble.

Twenty-four years ago, Martin was in a curious place with his career. More by accident and because of the shortage of jobs, he'd ended up in the rather bitter world of credit control. He worked alongside the credit control manager of a dominant Japanese consumer electronics company. They maintained their prestigious market profile by vetting customers extensively, offering them a credit line, and then jumping on them heavily if payments fell behind. In the most severe cases, the company and its representatives would go on what were lovingly termed 'snatch backs'.

A retention of title clause embedded in all delivery notes meant that the goods remained the property of the supplier until they were paid for in full. If this didn't transpire and the debt was sufficiently old, then the 'snatch' would be ordered in. Usually, a scout would be sent out on a preliminary mission to see what was available, in readiness for the later siege.

Martin's manager wasn't so keen on getting involved in this kind of aggravation, so he'd send one of his junior staff along on the premise that it was 'good experience for them', or some such nonsense. In reality, he was just very scared. Today, such a visit had been gifted to Martin.

Martin parked his Vauxhall Cavalier in one of the car parks on the outer fringes of the town. They often did this. It was a tactic. They were like special forces operatives but with TVs and audio gear. Working on the sometimes optimistic assumption that nobody would notice or recognise them, they'd have a steal on the situation, be able to recce the stock and any possible resistance ahead of their legalised smash and grab raid.

It had started to rain slightly just as Martin began his five hundred metre trek into the centre of the town. Strangely, it seemed to complement the place, adding another magnificent, dismal sheen to its marvellously miserable exterior. He reached the middle of the main street which ripped through everything, splitting the place almost equally in half. Both sides of the street were decked amply with bookmakers' shops and rough-looking pubs which had some of their windows obligatorily broken. He walked around a pool of dried blood which had stained most of one of the large paving slabs. It stood as a sort of diary, recording the drink-driven violence of the week before. Although the population was comparatively low in numbers compared with some other places, the inhabitants here were overly aggressive, and wilfully hurting each other seemed like some kind of local hobby, which they were all compelled to take up.

By the Betta Bargains shop, Martin looked across the road to his target. In fairness, the owner *was* trying. The windows of the shop were immaculately clean – apart from the stream of vomit down one side of them from the night before that is. The paintwork was fresh too, and its bright, resilient, eye-catching red colour blasted out for everyone to see. The windows were screened by a specialised metal mesh, which allowed you to peek through to the expensive and beautiful equipment beyond. This was the best that money could buy, state of the art; pure brilliance – but unfortunately still there, living in the window like some permanent squatter with no one willing to provide it with a home. Martin's face dropped as he spotted this. Possibly the situation was worse than they'd first thought.

Martin glanced up and down the deserted street and made his way across. A lone bicycle trundled along from the far end of town, the squeak from its pedals echoing off the enclosing walls. Martin tried the door handle of the shop first, and finding the entrance locked, he searched for a bell to ring. This was housed in a graceful intercom unit which was screwed to the wall at a comfortable height. It was like something from an exclusive club in the West End of London, protecting its posh clientele within from the prying eyes of the masses outside.

Martin pushed the shiny chrome button, and the tiny speaker below it hissed, almost sounding peeved. No voice came through it; rather, the latch on the door was simply released, with Martin now presumably having been examined and cleared by somebody viewing him from the other end of a camera somewhere. He pushed open the door and was instantly greeted by the attractive, thick-pile grey carpet which lined the entire floor beyond him. A young girl aged sixteen or so stood behind the counter. She said nothing as Martin entered – and looked half-bored and half-lost as she rattled around in the vacuous space all around her. Martin filled in the awkward silence for the benefit of both of them.

"Can I speak to Mister Carter please?" he asked.

"He's not here," the girl replied in her thick Midlands accent. "He's down at the Cove with his diving stuff," she went on to explain disinterestedly.

"When did he go?" Martin probed curiously.

The girl smiled sarcastically. "A few minutes ago," she confirmed and then grinned. "Just after he saw you arrive."

The Cove was a famous dive site located in an old flooded quarry. It was similar to the Pit in this regard but was substantially smaller. It was still deep and caused deaths but had nothing of the reputation of the Pit, which could be considered its competitor. Located seven miles from the audio shop, it was a relatively short drive for its owner.

As well as hosting a dive club, the Cove also had its own pub. This had long since carved out considerably healthy custom as a music venue, and it had the rather displaced look of a country and western club about it. When customers visited for the first time, they were greeted by an image of a snazzy gig in Texas, rather than an English public house located in the middle of Leicestershire. It was easy to understand how it had grown to what it had, however. It sat just above the level of the water, surrounded by the cliffs of the former workings. Performers could blast out their music without the risk of offending anyone save the fish and the few birds which lived there. This situation provided a superb advantage when it came to applying for licences from the local magistrates. Govern any drunken rowdies, and the issuing of this operational necessity was almost a certainty.

Martin parked up on the oddly shaped, elongated car park, which tracked the shore of the lake. He stopped for a moment, gathering his bearings when he spotted a lone figure down by the water's edge readying his gear. Close by was a freshly liveried new van with the letters AVS abundantly clear in a raging cherry colour. Connecting the obvious proximities, Martin advanced and then stopped a few metres short of the busying man.

"Excuse me," he began, "would you be Mark Carter by any chance?"

"Who's asking?" the man replied coldly and then he looked Martin up and down and smirked. "Of course I know who's asking," he continued, insultingly. "A suit in a place where suits don't belong – not those kind anyway."

"Then you probably know why I'm here?"

"Oh, I know. I've been expecting you for some time. You the manager – 'Davies' or 'Davy' then?"

"'David-son'. No, I work for him."

"Didn't want to come himself? Dumped it on you, has he? Spineless little shit."

"Part of the role, I'm afraid."

"Right: Tweedledee and Tweedledum. He's the one who sends out the letters and you're the one that collects things? We do talk in the trade, you know. Quite a reputation you've got between you."

"I tried the shop first. They sent me down here. We can go back there if you like."

"No, that won't be necessary, thanks."

"But can we talk?"

Mark grinned.

"No," he stated bluntly and turned away from Martin, making it evident he was ignoring him.

"Look, it might be better if we did," Martin persisted.

"No, that won't help much now, I'm afraid."

"Talking always helps surely, doesn't it?"

"Not always. It won't help with what I'm going to do anyway."

"And what's that then?"

Mark stopped what he was doing momentarily and turned back to face Martin.

"Have much influence in this 'role' of yours, do you?"

Martin thought for a moment. "I'm not sure I'm with you," he answered sounding bewildered.

Mark took a pace closer towards him. "Apart from money, it's influence, power that people want next. And so you should be very proud of yourself."

"Should I?"

"Yes, because you've got it in bucket-loads. You've got – you've *had* – much more influence in your tiny little role than you could ever have possibly imagined."

"And how does that work then?" Martin demanded, his tone indicating that he was getting more than a little tired of these apparent jibes now. Mark put down the regulator in his hand and moved to be face to face with Martin. There was threat in his countenance.

"You called me last week, remember? You talked about what would happen if I didn't pay? You do remember that, don't you?"

"Yes."

"About all the court action, the costs, no more stock, bankruptcy possibly?"

"That's what we talked about, yes."

"Good, I'm glad you remember," Mark replied and then thrust his face directly into Martin's. "Do you know what it's like to have no money at all? I mean NO money? No money – so you can't even eat?"

"Come on, it can't be that bad, surely?"

"You stupid little prick!" Mark blasted into him. "How the hell am I going to find fifteen grand in a week for you fuckers, do you think?" He moved away again now, laughing slightly. "After your call, I decided something," Mark continued and pointed at Martin viciously. "Because that's how much influence, how much *power* you've really got, you see."

"Is it?" Martin countered, getting more aggrieved now.

"Oh, yes, because I decided that if you *did* come visiting, then I'd do something about all this. I had a hunch you would – and you did. I saw you arrive, of course I did. Saw you eyeball the shop, check it out; park up. So, while you were meandering up the high street, I left by the back door and came down here." Mark hesitated and eyed Martin strangely. "Because I want you to witness this, to see the true consequences of all that *influence* you have."

"Witness what?" Martin battled on. He was finding the conversation difficult now. Mark grinned, and he stepped forwards to be closer to Martin once again.

"There's no way out of this for me – so it's simple," he began to explain. He pointed out to the middle of the lake. "I'm going to get into the water. I'm going to go out there, dive down to thirty metres – and then I'm going to turn my air off."

Martin was speechless at first. And then that moment; a fork in the road that suddenly looms up on you, and with no prior warning of its existence, there's a decision to be made, and all you can go on is your experience, your humility and your willingness to learn.

Given some of his current deficiencies, Martin went for the easiest option, the safe turn.

"You're joking," he quipped, clearly thinking Mark was bluffing.

"Right," was all Mark said, and he pivoted around, lifted his air tank, mounted it on his back and started to march into the lake. After ten or so paces, he spun back round to face Martin. His face was wet now with tears, and he daggered Martin with his finger as he pointed at him.

"*You* can tell my kids!" he bawled, and returned to his race into the water. Soon he was up to his waist.

Martin struggled now. All sorts of thoughts were racing through his head. He was unsure of what to do, equating what this man had just said to him, trying to rationalise his true suffering and now its possible consequences. In his mind he looked back down the route they were on in their conversation. He checked the distance they'd already travelled and calculated the effort he'd need to expend to backtrack and remap this whole episode, to forget his pride and avert that risk.

"Mark!" he yelled. Mark ignored him and carried on his way. By now his shoulders were under the water. He'd been fast and determined on his way there, almost unstoppable.

"Mark!" Martin called again, but Mark maintained his pace. "For God's sake stop!" Mark's regulator was in his mouth now. He was testing the flow and the valves, getting ready to submerge. And then one final try. "Look, I'm sorry, all right!" Martin screamed. Mark faltered slightly. "Let's talk, please!" Martin bellowed, sounding truly genuine now. "I mean *really* talk; properly, you know. Come on. Let me try and sort this for you!"

Mark stopped, hesitated, and then slowly took a step back towards the bank. He thought for a few more seconds and then continued on his way. Soon he was in the shallows again and finally on the shore. The two men stood and faced each other in silence for a while. Martin looked embarrassed, not certain about what to do next and so when the awkwardness became too much, he simply lunged forwards, took Mark by his shoulders and hugged him tightly.

"What the *fuck* have you been through?" Martin gasped. They were there for a good few seconds before either of them would let the other go.

Ten minutes later and they were in the bar of the pub supping a cold beer together. Martin had learned so much on what had started off as just another working day.

"Our lot have this thing; they call it 'can't pay or won't pay'," Martin elucidated. "It's how they decide what to do next. I've seen them write off debts if it's a 'can't'. They're really odd. It just means the credit manager has to write a letter of apology to the MD, accept the blame."

"What?" Mark exclaimed, taking another grateful slurp from his bottle.

"They *are* Japanese, don't forget," Martin qualified sarcastically.

"'Honour and all that shit?" Mark remarked and then looked soulful. "But he won't do that for me, will he? The miserable git."

Martin chuckled.

"He might if I tell him there's nothing here to take."

"Would you do that?"

"Why not," Martin replied, taking a swig too. "Always sending me out on crap I don't need. Like you said; should have come down himself, shouldn't he?" Martin grinned and chinked their bottles together. "Another?" he enquired enthusiastically. Mark didn't reply but rather just lowered his head down to the table top in a tangible display of relief.

"Thank fuck," he mumbled to himself. "Thank *fuck*."

Martin tapped him on his shoulder as if to console him, and then he stood and left for the bar. The bartender there greeted him with a warm smile.

"Another couple of Becks, please," Martin asked him keenly.

At Restaurant Jules in Menorca, Mark's coffee was cooling and he took a final sip. Carlos looked on from the shade indoors, and he seemed to pick up on his boss's distress. He quickly grabbed his tray and walked briskly back out on to the terrace to join him.

"Would you like another coffee, Mister Carter?" he asked considerately. "That one's nearly gone."

Mark peered up at him from his seat, and he appeared instantly welcoming and thankful. He'd obviously seen this kind man do this before; read a situation, add salvation, try and turn things around when there was absolutely no obligation for him to do so.

"No, Carlos," he replied softly. "I'm all coffee-ed out, thanks." He thought for a moment. "But do you know what," he went on, "I do rather fancy a beer though."

"Now that," Carlos acknowledged happily, "is something I *can* do," he said and trotted off eagerly back into the restaurant.

CHAPTER TWENTY-FIVE

The faint, blue glow of the neon from the radio mic provided enough light to reflect things back from the blackness outside; and there was a pair of eyes shining in from the glass of the mask. It's like scrying; when you gaze into a mirror for a long time and something possibly appears. People report seeing monsters or demons lurking there; some dark force ready to take over them. It must have been odd for her to have observed herself like this at such honest, close quarters, but whatever she glimpsed in that brief moment of self-examination, rather than deter her, it served to drive her on.

She circled for another time as if she was checking on her bearings, fixing where she was; preparing. Seeming happy that all was as it should have been, she spoke.

"Just for the log, I *am* on my own," she announced. "Right. So next time, come along." She sounded stronger all of a sudden. "Fuck it," Fiona declared. "This is me going for the record!"

Down at one hundred and forty metres, the light was curious. It appeared as if there was none, but there were still traces there, like long-forgotten memories in an ageing mind; all that is treasured still managing to force its way through. The odd, obstinate shaft bullied its way down from the surface like a high-calibre bullet, shot into the water, now rebelliously exceeding its range. In parts, there were shades of darkness, degrees; places not quite as consumed by their surroundings as others, sanctuaries of iridescence; patches of brightness travelling on their way through on the currents, like ghosts.

"It's just like Martin said it was," Fiona marvelled, the wonder contorting her voice. She looked to her side and then down into this strange new world all around her. "I can see the roads winding down, me floating above them," she continued. "It's surreal. The cranes, that big warehouse he talked about." She hesitated as she focused on something way off in the distance, propelling her body around with movements of her arms so she could get a better look. "My God, I've just seen the hanging tree," she exclaimed excitedly. "It looks *so* spooky – like it's swaying in a breeze."

She peered above her for a moment at the faint remnants of sky that simmered beyond all that massive weight of water, and then she returned to her immediate surroundings once again.

"The viz is better than I thought it would be, but he was right about the cold too," she said, a glaze of acceptance now in her tone. But then that changed. As she gazed below her, serious concern replaced her deceptive, previous calmness. "Deep now," she went on, "one-forty-five and still going down. But I'd be lying if I said I wasn't having difficulties though." She sounded instantly pained, a suffering wince with no accompanying words taking over the microphone now. But then that braver delivery: "Glad I decided to come," she stated proudly. "I've made all sorts of discoveries today – and they're all truly wonderful. Johnny, you would understand. Course you would," she continued somewhat obliquely. And then that stoical resolve, an admittance almost, the hint that she wasn't letting on that something awful was about to happen. "God," she said sounding totally amazed. "This place is so beautiful."

CHAPTER TWENTY-SIX

The traffic on the A55 Expressway heading to Wales was lighter than usual. It was mid-December, and the manic rush of the summertime getaways had lessened significantly. In a different season, the road would resemble the fatty, clogged arteries of a burger binger. Now it had more of the free-flow of an athlete about it; things were fluid, they could move, and the risks were lower. It helped that the weather was questionable too, and Fiona made good time as she headed comfortably on her way to the airport at Hawarden, positioned just over the border from England. Every so often she'd have to turn on her windscreen wipers as the heavens opened. She'd occasionally sneak a look skywards and pull a worried face as she glanced at the increasingly blackening clouds.

She was visiting the airport because one of her friends had bought her a trial flight for a birthday present at the flying school, which was based there. This was when she was twenty-nine, and her life still had an element of spontaneity about it. One casual remark while out on a drunken Saturday night with her chums about fancying flying, and here she was, zooming down to the region's largest aerodrome outside Liverpool or Manchester.

She found her exit and followed the road around the new and rather congested housing estates, past the neighbouring light industrial quarter and on towards the airfield. It was a huge place, an outcast from the Second World War with acres of spare land, which was gradually being developed; and one massive runway over a mile long. It had all the radar and instrument landing equipment of a major facility and was a designated field in which to bring jumbo jets and other seriously large civilian aircraft should they get into trouble and need to land in an emergency.

The security guard checked she was on the list of bookings, lifted the stout barrier and let her through. The main users of the field built aircraft on site and had military connections. They'd been the target of several terrorist attacks overseas, and so they were almost continuously on a status of red alert. The further she went into the location, the more Fiona felt she was entering a truly different world.

The road beyond the barrier weaved its way around the site, branching off at several places to feed some of the units, which were grouped together in various collections. These housed a mix of companies that made things for or serviced the aeronautical industry. Other units held offices, and the whole place had a feeling of affluence about it. After a further two hundred metres, Fiona finally reached the flying school. This was a smart affair too. It was situated in another new building which faced on to the 'air-side' part of the field. This was hallowed ground and was protected by big, heavy, locked gates, which were only accessed via carefully issued passes.

Fiona parked up in the car park by the side of the school and gazed out onto the land beyond the high, linked fence towering in front of her. This was where the planes lived and worked, and everything there looked terribly important. There were aprons and taxiways, and then cutting through the middle of it all, the huge runway itself. This ran at right angles some three hundred metres away from her with the remainder of it disappearing off into the distance to her right. At this end of the field, there was a control tower, high and commanding, which oversaw anything that happened beneath its all-powerful gaze.

Set halfway down the runway, off to one side, was a large orange windsock, which rather disturbingly was flying enthusiastically horizontally, its mass fully inflated, buffeting in the strong breeze, and facing perpendicular to the direction of the strip. Fiona looked away quickly as if this was something she didn't want to think too much about. She was no pilot, but she understood enough about speed and direction to know that possibly these weren't the best conditions in which to fly an aircraft.

This intuition was reinforced by what she saw in the aircraft park. The three two-seater Tomahawks and two four-seater Warriors were all neatly lined up on the apron nearest the school. What was most immediately evident was the lack of people. The place was largely deserted. The only things that moved were the wings of the aircraft as they rocked as the wind caught them and swayed them in unison, as another strong gust made its way through from the west.

The corridor to the flying school was adorned on either side by old photographs. They showed bombers and fighters from the last war, and on a couple of them, their crews were all lined up, proudly posing in front of them. They were all young and smiling. This fervour must have taken some mustering given what they knew they were likely to face; and the stark realisation that some of them might well be missing from any future photographs that were taken.

There was a young man on the reception desk of the school too, and in this regard, the past formed a seamless link with the present. He was friendly and greeted Fiona warmly, and she was grateful for the comfort this gave her. Just as he was starting the beginning of a conversation to see who she was and how he could help her, an older man entered and rudely cut across him. The older man was wearing a blue, crew-necked jumper with leather patches on its elbows. A small pair of aircraft wings were embroidered on the left-hand side of his chest. He strutted about officiously and had an annoying arrogance about him. Fiona smiled to herself. She'd joked on her night out about how she might meet a Tom Cruise look-a-like on her adventure in the skies. All she seemed to have encountered so far was a choirboy – albeit a very nice one – and Wallace from the *Wallace and Gromit* films.

"Will I be flying with you?" she asked the older man, trying not to offend him by sounding too disappointed. He glanced through the window to the weather outside.

"Oh no, not with me, love," he answered her with an oddly curious tone of relief in his voice. "You'll need somebody different to go up on a day like this. That'll be Johnny then, and he's here now," he indicated, looking past her through the open door of the office to the corridor beyond.

Johnny's hand was already outstretched as he approached Fiona. He was twenty-five and handsome with a cute, fashionable beard which hugged his features perfectly. He was a little over six feet tall and well-built. He wore smart black trousers and a beautifully-ironed white shirt, and over that, a tailored, red outdoor jacket. There were no wings embroidered anywhere, however. There was just a simple target emblem that gave a subtle reference to the RAF.

"Fiona?" he enquired, with a broad smile which showed off his even, ivory teeth.

"I think I'm a little early, sorry," Fiona almost babbled in reply, his appearance clearly still bowling her over a little.

"Don't be sorry," he answered her coolly. "Better to be early on a day like this. The weather's a little ropey, I'm afraid. It'll be a bit bumpy up there, but we'll be right enough." he reassured her confidently.

Johnny was the kind of person who seemed to have done everything early in his life. There were fewer boundaries he needed to break through as a result. He was naturally gifted at sports; he'd been a flying instructor since he was eighteen and coupled to that, was his love of adventure. He'd been a bush pilot in South Africa for a while and then been smitten by a volley of expeditions and taking on the impossible. He'd climbed Everest as if it had been a Sunday afternoon stroll, and now he was planning his next mission – a trek into a remote part of the Amazon where a lost tribe had supposedly been spotted. It was the stuff out of a Hollywood yarn, but it had captured his imagination.

After signing all the correct paperwork, which alarmingly included giving the name of Fiona's next of kin, they donned their florescent jackets and made their way out through the back of the clubhouse and on to Apron November. A blast of wind caught them as they exited the door and instinctively Johnny reached out to steady Fiona as she wobbled a little.

Up above them was a distinctly odd section of weather. To the south there were low-level clouds, their bases down at fifteen hundred feet or so. But to the north, there was a wall of rain which connected solidly with the ground. The whole pattern just sat there in situ as two air masses collided overhead and held it in place like invisible glue in the sky. Johnny inspected the increasingly darkening spectacle that was effectively dividing the airport into two halves.

"We'll go south," he quipped, considerately pointing to where south was in case Fiona didn't know, but also picking up on her concerned expression as she peered up at the sky.

The Warrior had four seats and a place to store luggage. It had a single engine and fixed propeller and a tricycle undercarriage. The technology was old; magnetos for ignition still, but this kind of kit could be timelessly depended upon, and so it superseded its modern rivals. Inside the cockpit there was a bank of dials, gauges and levers which were all designed to help fly the machine. Some of these included navigational instruments that would lock on to beacons and other ground-based aids that were littered around the country. GPS wasn't available in its full glory yet, but for airmanship and training, it would never be used in this aircraft in its entirety. The old skills of plotting courses and using visual references on the ground would prevail – and for one good reason. If everything turned to a ball of chalk, then you'd have this life-saver to rely on. If a pilot lost that skill, or was allowed to lose it by an over-reliance on new technology, then once the GPS went dead they would have nothing to get them home. Added to that would be the possibility of crashing into other aircraft or the occasional passing town or city beneath them, and the consequences of that would be too awful to comprehend.

Johnny stepped on to the wing of 'November Charlie'. He positioned his feet on the stronger parts of the structure which were detailed in grippy black paint. By now he'd already performed his A check which happened before the first flight of the day. He signed the log to say it had been completed and then slithered his way into the cockpit, sitting in the designated pilot's seat on the left-hand side of the aircraft.

"Come in, Fiona," he beckoned her, and she found the black markings as she'd been politely instructed to do, and then sat herself down in the seat next to him.

"Comfy?" Johnny asked, 'pinging' a lever down by the floor and moving her seat slightly forwards so she could reach the rudder pedals better. "There's no need to be nervous," he comforted her picking up on the anxiety she was wearing like a thick rouge on her face. He quickly flickered past the dials with his finger, seemingly conscious now that her condition was getting worse. "Don't worry too much about all these," he told her, "Just enjoy what we're going to do today and where we're going to go. I can tell you about what they do later." And then he turned to her and smiled serenely calmly. "You know, I think it's better if we just get on with it. What do you think?" he said. She nodded.

"Yes, okay," she replied, her voice now more than quivering a little. Johnny took her hand.

"It'll be all right," he said gently, and then faced forwards again, readjusted her headset so she could hear him fully and then, after running through the pre-take-off checks, he started the engine, woke up the radios and pressed the small black 'transmit' button on the side of the yoke in front of him.

"Hawarden Tower, good morning" he stated rather formally, "Golf, November, India, November, Charlie."

Five seconds later and the radio sang with the bright voice of the air traffic controller.

"Hawarden Tower, Golf, November, India, November, Charlie. Pass your message."

Looking happy with the quality of the reception, Johnny continued.

"Golf, November, Charlie's at Apron November. Request radio check and taxi for a local flight to the south as previously booked," he announced.

A few more transmissions followed and after taxiing, holding, conducting his power checks and then being given clearance to take off, they were lined up on the big, broad runway in front of them.

"Ready?" Johnny beamed, grinning over to her. Fiona nodded again as if she couldn't manage any more words. He opened the throttle, and the engine roared. He guided the direction of their ever-increasing acceleration by steering with his feet, and then he pulled gently back on the yolk and then they were airborne. The ground and its buildings, fields and roads grew smaller and smaller as they gained more height. Johnny pointed to the instruments when he saw Fiona looking at the massive black walls of clouds that were holding now, but only just, behind them.

"Don't worry," he reassured her. "I can fly on instruments in case they get too close. Relax. I'll get us home."

They headed south, skirting the base of the clouds and weaved around the feet of the high hills of Wales that rose up to the west. After ten minutes, Johnny faced Fiona with a grin.

"Your go now," he advised her flippantly.

She evidently thought he was joking.

"Don't be silly."

"No, it's true," he reaffirmed and briefly guided her through the controls. "Don't worry; it's all dual-operated, so nothing horrible is going to happen. But when I'm ready for you to fly her, I'll say, 'you have control', and you have to reply, 'I have control', just so I know you understand. The last thing we need is nobody flying this thing up here today. Is that okay?"

Fiona nodded once more, this time appearing a little overwhelmed. Johnny squeezed her left hand, which like her other one, was now gripping the yoke so hard the whites of her knuckles were showing through.

"Come, on, Fiona. You can do this. Of course you can." Another brief moment and then Johnny spoke again.

"You have control," he commanded.

After an initial hesitation, Fiona responded.

"I have control," she acknowledged, and the aircraft was hers.

November Charlie dipped quite violently at first, but after a few corrections, Fiona was flying virtually straight and level.

"Hey, look at this!" Johnny exclaimed. "You're doing brilliantly well!"

Fiona's face lit up as the magic of the situation took over her. Any sign of fear she'd had before had simply melted away.

"This is fantastic!" she cried as she gained more in confidence, "Really, *really* fantastic!"

After twenty more minutes of flying, they returned to the airfield. Johnny landed November Charlie with his usual excellence despite there being a seventeen-knot crosswind, which meant they came in on finals almost sideways. They taxied back to the apron and parked up. Johnny got approval from ATC to shut down, thanked them for their help and then switched the radios and the engine off. As he was finalising his post-landing checks, he turned kindly to Fiona after carefully removing her headset.

"So, did you enjoy that, Fiona?" he asked softly. She nodded enthusiastically.

"That was *so* good," she beamed.

Johnny smiled at her almost lovingly.

"Yes, it was, wasn't it?" he agreed. "Maybe we should do it again some time, what do you think?" he suggested.

Fiona had obviously connected with his intention. "Yes. Yes, I think we should," she said willingly as she stared deep into his eyes.

And that's how their relationship began, spawned by physics, terror, trust and exhilaration. They became indivisible after that. Fiona became the envy of her friends as she and Johnny transformed into the perfect couple together. And that's how it stayed for three happy years. The only condition Johnny had imposed on their relationship was to complete some of his expeditions. He'd fought so hard to get involved with them in the first place that some of the sponsors he'd managed to collect wouldn't disengage as easily as he could. He'd made it clear to Fiona that he wanted to settle down.

"You're my world now," he declared to her one evening right out of the blue. "I've already seen the other one."

All that remained was one last venture, one last obligation to the calling of his wild youth that he was now so happy to tame. Johnny had been on several jungle explorations before and was very well regarded. He'd be an obvious choice for the organisers. There'd been all sorts of hype about a lost tribe up the Amazon, and there'd been all sorts of failed attempts to find them too; so much so that many believed the whole thing was a hoax.

Hoaxes had been commonplace in the world of discovery before. They diluted the soup. They served to lessen the fear and the caution that it naturally generated. It might have been better if Johnny's trip had been to conquer a newly discovered face of the Eiger, because the real dangers of the encounter might have been more apparent, and the consequences better faced. But this wasn't the case. It almost felt as if they were setting off on some jolly; all that time and effort to simply finally unfrock some man from New England in his fifties dressed up, irreverently pretending to be indigenous.

And so Johnny prepared. He cut three months out of his life and got ready to go. Fiona saw him off from Manchester airport on a snowy February afternoon.

"I'll be waiting, love," were her last words to him before he blew a kiss and left; and sadly, she was.

After a month of no contact, everyone was beginning to become concerned. Some of the first of Johnny's party had already returned, but he'd moved forwards to set up an advanced camp. In the last radio call he'd made he'd said they'd discovered a part of the Amazon rainforest that 'no one had been to yet'; and then there was nothing. After three months, a rescue was ordered, but this proved fruitless. Another attempt to find him was made two months later. Six months after that and another search later, the assumption was made that Johnny and his two accomplices had perished in some way. Nobody was willing to say exactly how but no further searches were planned. The official line was that all attempts to find them had been exhausted. The unofficial line was that given how remote the area was and how expensive the past searches had proven to be, it was likely that the accountants had drawn a line under the whole affair and blamed it on the 'perils of adventure' or some other convenient financial escape route. They'd later state that 'these people knew what they were taking on', and that 'the danger was always there'. Because of these and other back-office evaluations, the tacit agreement seemed to be that there was nothing more anyone could – or would – do, and the whole operation was effectively closed.

Fiona was devastated and said that she would never give up hope. She always insisted that one day she'd get a call and there Johnny would be, smiling, happy; some plausible excuse in hand and back in her arms. But that never happened and as the years rolled on, the waiting took its toll on her. She was tormented by time. She was like some prisoner on death row getting a reprieve only for that to be subsequently withdrawn, and so she'd be left to sweat it out for a few more years until the whole thing came round on itself again. She hated time now because it toyed with her, and with each passing year there was less and less for her to hold on to. She became weaker and weaker. She was a desperate climber on a mountain seemingly reaching its summit only to find it was just another blind ridge and the trail ahead of her carried on and on.

It would have been so easy for her to have hated adventure too. That once-familiar friend who was so readily welcomed in, now exposed as a bitter enemy, having deceived her with its shiny lure of danger and risk. She became fearful of what lay ahead. She was like a detective searching for a missing person in the undergrowth, conscious that at any minute they might find something gruesome. Once she used to get a buzz from the mysterious and the undiscovered. Before, she'd had no problem with taking on the unknown, experimenting, trying anything new. But because her life had been mercilessly broken down to a meaningless repetition of false hopes and tease, she was now petrified of the very future itself, and like the detective, terrified of what could be lying there.

CHAPTER TWENTY-SEVEN

This was the part of her life that Fiona wouldn't necessarily have seen coming. It was a surprisingly smooth transition. There could have been the expectation that it wouldn't be, that there's a distinct separation between the states; that you disembark from one train, walk along the platform and board another one. But what if you simply walked through to the next carriage; a simple sliding door and that's it?

Fiona found herself now in a totally different place. It was more or less undefined. It had a cream-coloured hue about it. There were no walls to see or touch, no horizon to look out to or fix on, no smells particularly. It was like a gigantic balloon, and she was there inside it, mixed in with the air like any other substance. There was only the soft and comforting present. It carried the feel of a happy Christmas morning. It was a place where joy dwelled; a place of contentment and peace.

Fiona looked about her anxiously trying to rationalise it all, but it was clear that she was unable to. And just before her growing fear developed into sheer panic, she saw something off in the near distance coming towards her. After a few seconds of studying, trying to make out what it was, she took a nervous step backwards in complete disbelief.

"Congratulations," Martin said kindly as he walked closer into view. "You made it down."

Dazed. That moment when excessive alcohol hits, when you're witness to an accident and the whole world slows down.

That point thirty seconds after the anaesthetic has been administered and all reality is forcibly removed from you. Fiona was lost. She questioned her sight as an immediate response, screwing at her eyes with her curled-up fingers, utterly convinced she was seeing something else and not this image before her.

"What?" she spluttered distractedly.

Martin took another step.

"They got it," he continued, "the depth, the evidence; everything." Fiona still looked hopelessly confused. "All the way down to the bottom, love."

Fiona glanced quickly about her; scrutinising everything, still searching for clues, something to make sense of all this.

"I … I still don't understand," she stammered. Martin hesitated and then walked up to her, so they were face to face.

"You made it, Fiona," he announced affectionately. "You're the first one down. You got the record." He looked away for a moment, and his voice became more serious all of a sudden. "But then all the gauges just … fell away."

"Sorry?" Fiona burbled, but now obviously sure that Martin was something or someone she could actually communicate with. He appeared saddened now.

"Don't you remember what happened?" he asked an element of pity in his tone.

A flash of horror rippled suddenly across Fiona's face.

"Where's my mask?" she cried, frantically feeling for it.

"You got trapped in the cables on the bottom."

Fiona checked for her weight belt. She looked down at her legs.

"Where's my bottles; my suit!" she screamed.

"You ditched them," Martin explained, sounding pained now. "You tried to wriggle free before your air ran out."

Fiona spun around in a full circle, her eyes savaging everything.

"Where's the water?" She turned to Martin just as rapidly. "Come on: where's the water for God's sake!" Martin didn't answer. Fiona instantly froze. "Where the hell are we, Martin?"

Martin smiled kindly, like someone does ahead of breaking unspeakably bad news.

"Not where we used to be," he replied reservedly.

Fiona inspected Martin now, picking at his features as she fought harder for answers to the questions that threatened to overwhelm her. Martin didn't appear frightened but wore an intriguing mixed expression of both melancholy and exploration. He was like a freshman on their first day at college; he was homesick but expectant and curious too.

"It's doesn't have to be bricks and mortar, Fiona," he carried on obscurely. "Just because you didn't realise that room in your house existed doesn't mean it isn't there."

Fiona glared at him.

"Where are we, Martin!" she demanded.

"The police divers only work to a safe operational limit of fifty metres. You were much, much deeper than that; and so they couldn't recover you."

Fiona turned away suddenly as her brain began to race, as she started to connect a jumble of previously disjointed facts.

"Jesus," she moaned and began to sink to the floor as some new construction materialised in her head. "Oh my God! Sweet Mother of God! What's happened to me!" she yelled.

Crippled by her realisation, she stumbled forwards. Martin moved in to catch her in his arms, but she pushed him away.

"This can't be happening," she wailed. "It *can't be!* This is a dream. This is a nightmare or something?"

Martin shook his head.

"This isn't a dream."

Fiona stood tall again, posturing in front of him like an opponent in a bar fight. "Hit me then and prove it isn't."

Martin shuffled awkwardly, clearly not wanting to.

"Hit me!" she repeated.

Martin reached out and gently touched her cheek. "It's *not* a dream, Fiona," he assured her softly.

"Then I'll hit you."

Before he could dodge her blow, Fiona slapped Martin hard across his face. The sound of the impact affected her too, but more heavily so, and she immediately squatted down low to the ground as another wave of certainty crashed into her, weakening what remaining resistance she had left.

"This can't be true!" she bawled. Martin stared down at her, his silence more effective than any words he could have spoken. Fiona wailed again:

"No ... no ... no ...!" And suddenly she rose to her feet, confronting Martin furiously. "Why did you make me do it? Why did you make me go!"

Martin took a precautionary step back. "Technically, I didn't," he answered her calmly. "I wasn't there, remember?"

"You know what I mean; the concept, the idea, the desire then? You piece of shit!"

"You decided completely on your own."

She lunged at him. "You bastard! You fucking, fucking bastard!"

Martin grabbed her flailing hands, restraining her, and slowly her attack faded and as it did, Martin consoled her. What replaced the violence now however, was something far more destructive. Fiona was petrified again, and she began to moan.

"No ...!"

"There's no need be frightened, Fiona."

"Why!" Fiona snapped hatefully. "Why is there 'no need to be frightened', you prick?"

"Life's had its fair share of torment from you already."

"Holy fuck. I NEVER wanted this!"

"It can't take a chunk of your life when you've spent years worrying about how it ends, and then when the end of that road *is* finally reached, expect a continuation of that torment too."

Fiona gained space, looked into his face. "And that means what, exactly?"

Martin smiled again as if he was trying to help her comprehend.

"It was as if you just fell asleep. It was almost beautiful."

"Wonderful," Fiona scoffed cuttingly.

"But it was peaceful too, comforting."

Fiona almost laughed. "'Comforting'? Are you fucking-well kidding me!"

"But that's the point."

"And why is that!"

Martin waited a second before answering her. "Because it will be," he said.

"My God." Fiona's desperation hadn't waned. "I really *can't* believe this is happening." But then she was lighter; there was hope in her voice. "But it's not, is it?" she giggled. "This is a joke. This is one of your wind-ups, right?" She frantically looked about her as if trying to spot people. "Where are they? Are they hiding? You're all in on this, aren't you? Everyone in the club, taking the piss – you bunch of fucks!" And then she stopped as a stout barbed-wired fence of logic halted her track. "But how can it be?" she mumbled and gazed into Martin's eyes. "You died."

All traces of relief deserted Fiona now. In a sense, she awoke. The dream had ended, and as it did, it forced her to escape, to find a place to hide. It was a basic human instinct; the fighting done, now flight the only thing remaining; seeking safety as that vital final action.

She ran a few paces away from Martin and sat down, tight in a ball, sobbing as the veracity consumed her.

"Where are we, Martin?" she prodded timidly after a short while. Martin took his time to answer, choosing his words.

"Suppose these things are classified, graded?" he began delicately. "Suppose there's a kind of evolution to it – but not necessarily as you'd expect. Had you not taken that risk, would you actually be here?"

Fiona stood again and shrieked, "Where's *here*!"

Martin smiled.

"It's a wonderfully gentle place. People think these two worlds are eons apart, but they're not. If this *were* bricks and mortar, then they'd be like very cheap flats. The walls between them are incredibly thin. But like I said, you shouldn't be frightened."

"Well, you're wrong, you know, absolutely wrong because I *am* frightened, in fact, I'm fucking petrified."

"But do you?"

"Do I what?"

"*Do* you feel frightened? Do you feel 'petrified', really? Or is that how you think you should feel? How you used to feel? Is it just an old response; something that's outdated now? Take a moment to think. Like sniffing the air on the first day of spring: that scent of the newly blooming flowers, that softness on the breeze, the hint of something 'nice' ahead after all those dark, cold, hateful weeks you've had to endure."

Fiona uncoiled a little as she considered what Martin had said. She appeared instantly more at ease.

"No," she admitted reluctantly. "No, I don't feel frightened."

"And you *have* earned it – this peace – by what you did." Martin looked at her wisely. "Do you understand your grandmother any better now?" He caught Fiona's attention, and she turned to face him. "Is she clearer, more real; like a shadow gone?"

Fiona pictured something in her mind and her expression brightened just a little. She peered about her oddly, as if she believed that someone might suddenly appear.

"It's almost as if she's here," she murmured fondly.

"We've all watched those David Attenborough programmes about 'life', haven't we?" Martin went on. "And we say 'Yes, I get it, I understand'. But when do those systems, those drivers actually stop?"

Fiona lost her temporary sheen of serenity for a moment.

"Don't go all weird on me, Martin," she croaked. "Just tell me what happens next."

Martin pondered.

"I don't know. I haven't been here long enough to determine that."

"You don't know?"

"No."

"Great."

Fiona lowered her head, visibly frustrated by this apparent lack of information. Martin looked away and gazed into the distance as he spoke.

"I always feel sorry for flies with spiders," he mused, "that awful way to die. They can't flee; escape. All that, sticky ness, being trapped, unable to move, held there, the web so thin it's like an invisible force. And then their insides get sucked out while they're probably still alive. I can think of better things to do. But then I wondered if that cruelty is somehow returned."

He took a moment and then carried on.

"I saw them in my bath one afternoon. I came in too late to stop the bout; two big, leggy monsters, facing up to each other, all other available resources gone due to the season – Winter and no grub. Both of them suddenly finding themselves as the next 'ready meal' and having to fight it out to prove nature's point. Trouble is there was only one meal being taken away from that fast food outlet on that particular chilly afternoon. But it was as if they both knew it too. It was truly horrible. The cruelty fed on itself in that dreadful irony of supply and demand as they battled it out, and one won and one didn't, and one fed

179

and the other couldn't. Well, that's not us. We're not in that chain anymore."

Martin addressed Fiona directly again. "I stopped," he confessed, "I came back for you."

Fiona appeared unsure of what he meant.

"Why? Why did you 'come back for me'?" She glanced about her. "Wherever I am."

For the first time in the last few months, Fiona now studied Martin as if he was totally sincere.

"Because I'm your dive buddy, aren't I?" he declared proudly. "That's what buddies do. They look out for each other, take care of each other, protect; sacrifice for each other possibly in the most extreme cases."

Fiona relaxed a little, almost as if she knew the answer to her question before she presented it.

"And is this an extreme case?" she asked cautiously.

Martin grinned.

"I'd say it probably is, wouldn't you?"

Fiona still appeared uncomfortable, but also now a little more resigned.

"Shit. So, you really *don't* know what's ahead?" she commented somewhat despairingly. "Please don't tell me that you're winging it like you usually do?" She thought, identified her error and corrected herself. "Like you usually did?"

"Oh, I'm winging it all right, but sometimes that gets the best results. And anyway, this seems like the kind of place where you can do that sort of thing."

Fiona became suddenly upset again as his reference to a 'place' seemed to ravage her. Martin approached her and opened his arms offering her a hug. She resisted initially and then she fell into them, crying softly on his shoulder for a while.

"Just treat it like your first major dive," Martin advised her caringly. "They're pretty much the same emotions I guess; the challenge, the thrill, the terror and then the 'what the hell'."

"Like your Solomon Islands?"

"And your Menai Straits. Raging against the currents, ripped halfway down the coast by them but still in total control; disappearing under the waves, worrying the holidaymakers looking on half to death. Hey, and look on the bright side; at least we both don't have to deal with that silly wanker at the council any more."

"Yeah, there is that, I suppose," Fiona remarked philosophically. Then she broke from their embrace and forced a painful smile.

"If only she could see us now, eh?" she quipped.

They shared the image and then a laugh together. When it had passed, they both sank into a moment of contemplation again.

"Have you finally worked out where you are?" Martin probed gently.

Fiona's lip quivered a little. "Is it *really* all over, Martin?" she asked him desolately.

"Or all just beginning? Why does it bother you; all this uncertainty, the unknown? Why should it bother you *now* given how you've beaten everything? Just think about what you've done, Fiona, where you've been; why you're here."

Fiona considered his words and grinned suddenly.

"Bloody hell," she exclaimed, "did I really get the record?"

"Yes, you did – and absolutely on your own. Now you can legitimately say" – Martin painted a banner in the air with his hands – "the Incident Pit – I've totally shit on that!"

Fiona settled again.

"Then I guess it shouldn't bother me, should it?" she ruminated. "But it's been a pretty stressful afternoon."

"You know, it might just be that those won't exist anymore."

"Perhaps."

Martin deliberated for a few moments and then appeared as if he wanted to move; to shift their position.

"This shouldn't be that hard for a couple of brave souls like us," he began again, "for a brave soul like your grandmother." Fiona smiled. She looked at peace. "Like Rob."

Fiona reacted instantly to this mention of his name.

"Rob?"

Martin smiled and offered her his hand, and she took it willingly.

"Come on, Fiona," he continued, "it's just the next dive, isn't it? Let's go and explore this amazing new place together."

With no more words spoken, Martin took a pace forwards, and only after hesitating slightly, Fiona followed. Hand in hand they walked comfortably on their way together, heading into a distance that they couldn't see beyond. Soon the light changed, and after a few more steps, it absorbed them. The soft mist that had formed dissipated – and then they could be seen no more.

THE END